ELVIS
vs
HITLER

(ELVIS IS ALIVE, IV)

A Novel of Love, Duty and Honor

FOREWORD

Elvis Presley is unique among the world's enetertainers. Never before has any performer been kept "alive" by their legions of fans to the extent that Elvis has.

This novel is a look at Elvis Presley's unique place in history and his seeming immortality. We hope that his family and his millions of fans will appreciate this novel for what it is: a speculative look at the phenomenon that is Elvis.

Editor's note:
ELVIS vs. HITLER (ELVIS IS ALIVE 4)
is a work of <u>fiction</u>. The Elvis Presley Estate has not sanctioned this book.

This novel is dedicated to
Elvis fans all over the world.

Long Live The King.

CHAPTER ONE

"No…. it can't be you…! "It simply cannot be you !!!!!!!!!"

"NO…. Dr. Robert St. John… I absolutely WILL NOT ALLOW it to be YOU…... !!!" came the astonished, agonized and incredulous voice of the King of Rock 'n Roll…… Elvis Presley.

"I simply won't allow this to start again," that incensed famous voice shouted. "I CAN NOT… WILL NOT… go through all this again!" Elvis yelled, shaking his long rich dark black hair forcefully and repeatedly to emphasize his resolve.

I immediately noticed the fullness and thickness of his hair, and assumed it was resulting from hair dye because of his age. There were crinkles around his eyes, but all in all, Elvis Aaron Presley looked incredibly well, especially for a man who supposedly died over 20 years ago. Of course, there was that omnipresent sneer in his lip.

Dr. St. John, "Elvis exclaimed sighing, again shaking his dark-haired head in incredulity as he walked directly toward me.

"It was my belief the last time I saw you in Paris…" said Elvis stopping right in front of me, standing in a manner that reminded me of the pictures I saw of him when he was serving in the US Military, "…that there would be no more unexpected visits," then, taking a stern step toward me, "…that there would be no more questions."

"No more. NONE of THIS" Elvis exclaimed demonstrably, crossing his hands in a negative manner in front of him and shaking that jet black hair covered head to and fro, showing he did not approve of my presence in his Monte Carlo home.

Then Elvis looked up at me and his eyes began to 'twinkle'. "Dr. St. John, did anyone ever tell you that you look like Charlton Heston when he starred in *The Ten Commandments ?!*

"Almost every day, Elvis!" I exclaimed, smiling broadly at the dramatic change in Elvis' attitude as he broke out in a small laugh at my unexpected appearance at his Monte Carlo home.

"Well, come on in, Dr. St. John, and explain to me what you are doing in the vacation capitol of the world……Monte Carlo !!!"

"Let me tell you, Elvis…"   I'm looking for you, brother!" I laughed, and could literally feel my bright blue eyes twinkling with joy, realizing Elvis was glad to see me and had invited me into his exotic seaside townhouse.

I walked into the cavernous front room of a palatial living room, immediately thinking to myself, "this is like Graceland, but in Europe." Even the walls were decorated with everything Elvis; ornate outfits, gold records, movie posters, photos of family, two guitars.

"Hey that one is my favorite!" I yelled as I pointed to a poster from the movie, **Blue Hawaii**. I couldn't help it ….I started a rendition of the song **Beach Boy Blues**: *"Minding my own business, drinking my daddy's juice, I swear I will never touch that stuff again !!!!!!!!!!"* all while giving a guitar-playing rendition with both hands and swinging my hips in my 'best' attempt at an Elvis Presley impersonation.

Elvis held up his right hand, waving at me to immediately stop my incantation of the song, shaking his dark black hair covered head in a negative manner. "Stop, Dr. St. John, and please, never quit your day job to be a singer!"

I couldn't help it, as I had to guffaw and snicker at The King of Rock 'n Roll's comment.

"Yep, that was a great movie, Dr. St. John! I loved filming it in Hawaii, it is such a beautiful place!" Elvis proclaimed again waving his right hand exuberantly up in the air reiterating his love for the island of Hawaii and nodding his head fervently up and down demonstrating his glee in remembering the filming of such a great movie.

"Elvis, WHO are you talking to?" came a woman's accented voice from behind a sliding glass door that led to an adjoined opulent bedroom.

"Just an old friend!" Elvis declared to the beautiful brown haired goddess who poked her head around the door, her hand holding on firmly onto the door.

"OK, darling," she replied, smiling broadly as the gorgeous unknown lady slung her massive auburn locks and then disappeared back into the bedroom.

Noting the big smile on my face, Elvis explained, "that is Katarina, my woman," then nonchalantly tilted his head to the side, mirroring my smile.

"Elvis, she seems to be a very nice lady."

"Dr. St. John, Katarina is gorgeous.!" Elvis proclaimed emphatically.

"Yes, Elvis, very much so!" I replied, confirming the obvious.

Elvis then reached and grabbed me by both shoulders and gently directed me to a very large green velour couch in front of a massive granite stone fireplace. Above the fireplace was a classic Elvis picture from the early 60's showing him in a form-fitting shining black velvet suit, legs in a classic stance, holding his Gibson guitar. I could not help but noticing and had to remark, "By the way, Elvis, you have lost all that extra weight you had gained."

"Thank you, thank you very much!" Elvis stated in an almost pseudo-parody of his classic voice, large smile on his face. Then, losing his smile, Elvis' gaze turned toward the ceiling. "Of course I lost all of that weight!" He continued to talk upward as if explaining to himself as much as to me. "Gaining all of that weight was just a ruse to help get me out of my life …..."

Elvis clapped his hands boldly together and then dropped them to his side, using them to brace himself as he plopped down beside me on the plush green sofa, shaking his head in a negative manner showing that he was not going to join me into returning to his former life that we had before.

"So…… what brings you here to the playground of the French Riviera, Monte Carlo?" Elvis sighed.

I pouted my lips and shook my head in agreement with Elvis signaling that I was going to impart to the King of Rock 'n Roll what I was doing in his villa in Monte Carlo when a few years ago had decided I was gonna leave him alone.

"Elvis," I breathed in deeply and exhaled, waving my right hand high in the air above my head trying to signal only good intentions; "I have to know a couple more things." Elvis' eyes grew huge in hysterical disbelief as he slung his long black locks back and forth as a further sign of incredulity.

"Dr. St. John, I thought you swore to me the last time you had learned all you had to know and your saga in looking into my life was complete!!"

"Elvis…baby…" came an interruption, "tell Dr. St. John the whole story like you told me!" The shapely brown haired consort jumped from behind the door and into the room and stood directly in front of Elvis and me. It was the beautiful Katarina, waving her right index finger, commanding Elvis to tell me everything.

Elvis sat there with his mouth agape, not knowing what to say or do. Katarina stood there defiantly, shaking her luxurious thick dark brown tresses back and forth in a 'well, we are waiting…' stance.

Elvis sighed and looked first at me then back at the anticipatory Katarina. "OK, Kitty Kat." Elvis exhaled and sighed, calling his woman by her nickname. Calling her by her 'Kitty Kat' nickname elicited an exaggerated 'ELVIS!' from Katarina, tilting her head so that her thick mane touched her right shoulder.

I felt I needed to intercede to prevent further drama between the two lovebirds. "There is one overriding issue that I want to resolve!" I sighed, exhaling loudly in order to attract Elvis and Katarina's attention. He swiveled away from Katarina and turned around toward me. Directing his gaze straight at me, his mouth agog, that trademark sneer in his lip.

Instinctively Elvis threw his hands up in a 'So,…what IS it?' gesture.

"President Nixon," I remarked, holding up my hands, mirroring Elvis' previous, 'what is it" gesture.

"Yes, baby," Katarina interceded, walking directly toward Elvis and plopping her curvaceous body next to a still open-mouthed Elvis, directing her gaze deep into Elvis' eyes, "Tell Dr. St. John about how all this began with your meeting with President Nixon!" Katarina nodded her head up and down, emulating Elvis' wide open expression. "Please baby, tell the doctor about your meeting with President Nixon just like you told me!!!" She smiled, reaching over and patting Elvis on his knee. The brown haired beauty exuded, "Tell Dr. St. John the whole wild, crazy, UNBELIEVABLE story!!"

CHAPTER TWO

Elvis shook his ebony hair and exhaled in exasperation as he looked over at me! "Charlton Heston …. OOPS!! I mean Dr. St. John…"

Elvis began to reveal his frustration about again having to go back deeply into his life story, a life he must have felt he had left far behind, as he momentarily gazed at the gorgeous Katarina, who massaged his knee with silent compassion. Clearly Katarina sensed the frustration building in Elvis, as she began to gently pat The King of Rock 'n Roll on that same right knee. Elvis looked over at his emotional benefactor and emitted a loud, deep and prolonged sigh. Katarina leaned over and planted a firm kiss on Elvis's cheek with her luscious lips, then tilted her head and peered into Elvis' eyes with orbs as deep and dark blue as the ocean just outside their door. "Go ahead, Elvis," she said, leaning slightly forward and kissing Elvis lightly on his lips. Peering even more intently into his eyes, she coaxed, "Tell Dr. St. John about your meeting with President Nixon at the White House." Katarina purred, looking ever deeper into the King's eyes. "Explain to Dr. St.. John what that eventful White House meeting led your life to."

Elvis sighed deeply again, and with an expression of resignation on his face began to slowly move his head up and down in the affirmative. "Okay baby…." Elvis murmured as he smiled at Katarina, "I'll do it for you."

"BUT NOT BECAUSE YOU SHOW UP UNIVITED ON MY DOORSTEP, BUSTER!!!!" Elvis exploded as he tore his gaze away from the beauty queen and peered at me square in the face, stabbing his right index finger directly at me. But fortunately for me, a smile began to carve up that lip with the famous sneer, showing to me that he was not really angry or perturbed at my sudden intrusion into his new life on the Northern coast of the Mediterranean Sea.. He was simply surprised by my unexpected reappearance.

"Thank you, thank you very much, Mr. Presley," I blurted out as I flashed a huge glistening white smile revealing my appreciation to the 'King of Rock 'n Roll'.

Elvis sighed again in resignation that he would have to reach back in his distant memory and retell his story yet again. Whether Elvis knew it or not, his meeting with President Richard Nixon was very, very intriguing, and as it turned out, whether they were aware or not, monumentally important to the average American citizen. Elvis' smile revealed to me once more that he was not angry …..just that he would have to 'return' back in his memory so, he could rehash the intricacy of his historic Presidential meeting without fumbling and stumbling in the dialogue.

Katarina kept patting Elvis' right knee in re-assurance, repeating over and over again in a tone barely above a whisper, "Go ahead, Darling, tell Dr. St. John about your very first meeting with President Nixon in the Oval Office at the White House." Her knee patting becoming more intense, reassuring 'The King' that the story would go smoothly.

"Where should I begin?" Elvis smiled broadly. "It was a dark and rainy night…" The 'King' humorously mimicked the story with a tongue-in-cheek jab at the way so many novels by amateur writers is started.

"STOP IT, ELVIS!" Katarina snorted, trying her best to hide her accent, playfully slapping Elvis hard on his right knee showing her dissatisfaction, but her broad smile belied her humor in his 'joke'. Tilting her head and declaring again, doing her best to mimic her accented English, "ELVIS, tell Dr. St. John the story of you meeting President Nixon in the Oval Office of the White House!" Then opening her eyes widely, Katarina exclaimed, "It's important !!!!"

Elvis sighed, leaned back into the richness of the green velour sofa and mustered an acquiescent ...... 'OK' ....

CHAPTER THREE

"Welcome, Mr. Presley, to the White House," the crisply starched black tuxedo-clad butler announced to the 'King of Rock 'n Roll.'

Elvis Presley walked further up into the foyer outside of the Oval Office and explained, "Please sir, call me ELVIS. No one calls me Mr. Presley." Elvis smiled and continued taking time to pat the Butler on the shoulder in a friendly fashion, "Mr. Presley is my father, Vernon."

"I understand Mr.….er…. I mean Elvis" the butler responded, managing a smile through his 'starched' persona. Elvis smiled and said, "Great" revealing the famous sneer.

"Thank you, thank you very much.!" The butler retorted, which drew a soft chuckle and a large smile from Elvis.

Suddenly the doors to the Oval Office swung open and a lovely blonde haired lady emerged, smiling broadly.

"Mr. Presley, The President will see you now," she announced, bowing her head slightly in deference to the 'King of Rock 'n Roll.'

The butler, aware of the protocol, politely stepped aside and extended his open hand in a 'you may enter now' gesture, and stated while bowing his head in respect, "Thank you, Mrs. Nixon." Nodding his head toward the First Lady, he turned and walked away briskly.

Elvis smiled broadly as he recognized Patricia Nixon, First Lady of the United States of America. "First Lady, please, It is Elvis." Elvis smiled broadly and held himself upward in respect and reiterated. "No one calls me Mr. Presley. Mr. Presley is my father , Vernon."

"Of course, Elvis!!" Pat Nixon exuded with a large smile on her face "I am your biggest fan!"

"You ain't nothing but a Hound Dog, cryin' all the time…" came a voice from behind a huge swivel chair behind the stately Oval Office desk. The smiling face of President Richard Milhous Nixon appeared as the large chair rotated slowly to face Elvis. The President suddenly jumped out of

his chair began to rotate his hips and knees à la The King of Rock 'n Roll. President Nixon stopped his 'Elvis' gyrations, smiled broadly and extended his right hand to grasp Elvis' hand. "Great meeting you, Mr. Presley." Elvis and the President shook hands firmly while standing on the impressive rug emblazoned with the Presidential Seal.

"It's Elvis, Mr. President. No one calls me Mr. Presley," Elvis sighed, repeating his admonition that he preferred to be identified by his first name. Pat then stepped forward and grasped her husband by his right elbow. She smiled at him while tilting her head slightly, explaining and gently nodding, "This is Elvis, Dick." Still grasping the President's elbow, she stated, "Elvis does not respond to Mr. Presley. Mr. Presley is his father Vernon's name."

The President turned his gaze away from Pat and looked Elvis straight in the eye as he continued to shake Elvis's hand. "Alright then, Elvis," President Richard Nixon declared emphatically, "Call me Dick!"

Elvis and the President continued to shake hands enthusiastically and both turned their smiling gazes to their hostess, Pat Nixon.

Elvis finally broke his eye contact with Pat and Richard Nixon and began to look around the Oval Office and declared, "This place is even greater and more magnificent than what is shown in all the pictures!"

President Nixon nodded in agreement as he directed his gaze to the artifacts and memorabilia positioned everywhere around the Oval office.

"Yes, Elvis," President Nixon proclaimed, waving his right hand around the room. "This place is wonderful, full of history." The President took a step off the center of the rug showcasing the magnificent Presidential Seal. "Just look at this beautiful emblem we are standing on."

The First Lady recognized the oncoming all too familiar diatribe that her husband was going to launch into explaining the fascinating history of the Oval Office. Not wanting Elvis to be delayed for hours by endless stories relayed by her husband explaining the historical relevance of their surroundings, Mrs. Nixon stepped forward, looking solemnly into his eyes, and once again grabbed her husband by the arm, twisting it back and forth to maintain his attention. "Dick, why don't you tell Elvis why you have invited him here to the White House!"

President Nixon looked at his wife and then at Elvis, tilted his head as if to freeze a thought in place. He held up his right index finger, "But first, Elvis, would you like to have some lunch here in the Oval office?"

Elvis glanced quickly at Pat, then back at the President and nodded his head in agreement that he indeed would like to have something to eat.

The President peered at his wife, and she too was nodding her head up and down in agreement with lunch in the Oval office.

"Ok, then!" President Nixon clapped his hands together in delight that he was going to be able to treat the 'King of Rock 'n Roll' to lunch. "Elvis, you want a fried peanut butter and banana sandwich?" he asked rhetorically with his head cocked quizzically.

Elvis laughed out loud. "Yes, Mr. President, a fried peanut butter and banana sandwich will be wonderful…as long as it is made with JIF peanut butter!!

President Nixon leaned over the desk and pressed a button on the intercom. "Anna, would you be so kind as to bring Mr. Presley, er.. Elvis… a fried peanut butter and banana sandwich, MADE with JIF peanut butter, please!!!"

"Yes Mr. President," came the delighted voice of the kitchen chef. " Also, shall we bring you and Mrs. Nixon your lunch favorites?"

"Yes, Anna, bring us our favorites from McDonalds!!" the President giggled. As he turned back to Pat and Elvis, he saw Elvis holding his side, trying hard not to laugh. "What is SO funny, Elvis ?!?!"

"McDonalds?" Elvis quizzed between laughs. Both the First Lady and the President looked at each other and shrugged. "Yes Elvis, we LOVE McDonalds!" the First Lady added, tilting her head in bewilderment at Elvis finding so much humor in their choice of lunch.

"You are the President and the First Lady of the United States of America!" Elvis continued to hold his side as he laughed heartily. "You two have a whole stable of the finest chefs and cooks on the planet. You can have anything for lunch you want!! But you both order McDonalds ?!?!"

The First Lady crossed her arms defensively over her chest. "ELVIS AARON PRESLEY…The President and I absolutely LOVE McDonalds, and besides, anyone who eats fried peanut butter and banana sandwiches certainly has no room to talk!"

With that snappy comeback from the First Lady, Elvis, blushing with embarrassment, nodded his head contritely. "Please don't misunderstand, I LOVE McDonalds too. It's just that you two could have anything you want….!"

"McDonald's IS what we want!" Pat Nixon interjected as she looked at her husband, President Nixon. The President looked back at his wife with a look and a quick nod that confirmed agreement.

"I am changing the subject," Mrs. Nixon said as she took a couple of steps toward Elvis, "how did you like being in Germany, in the Military?"

"I liked Germany……being in the Military was good." Elvis responded smiling.

"Knock, knock; lunch is ready, Mr. President" José Martinez, the tuxedoed waiter, pushed a silver cart into the Oval office. José bowed slightly as he pulled the shiny domed silver cover off the cart to reveal three gold lunch plates. "The usual for the President and First Lady" José proclaimed in his Hispanic accented English as he presented plates with McDonald's burgers and French fries to President and Mrs. Nixon.

After eloquently presenting the Nixon's sumptuous lunch, José turned to Elvis. "And for the King of Rock 'n Roll," José bowed deeply and presented Elvis with his gold plate. "A fried peanut butter and banana sandwich… made exclusively with JIF peanut butter!" José bowed slightly at the wait as he took a courteous step back toward the door.

"Thank you, sir!" Elvis smiled and waved broadly at the friendly waiter.

"Anything else?" José asked, turning to the President and the First Lady.

"No José, that is everything." The President smiled between bites of his cheeseburger. The trio quickly turned to consuming their lunch.

"This is GREAT!" Elvis proclaimed. "José and team are great…they definitely put JIF peanut butter on this sandwich" "

You can tell the difference, Elvis?" "Pat Nixon quizzed.

"Absolutely, Ma'am, JIF peanut butter is just better!" Elvis nodded his head in agreement with his own declaration as he took the last bite of his fried JIF peanut butter and banana sandwich.

President Nixon took the last bite of his McDonald's cheeseburger and slapped his hands together as if he was cleaning them. Instantly, Pat Nixon mimicked her husband, crushed the wrapper from her McDonald's cheeseburger and slapped her hands in an 'I'm finished also' fashion.

Elvis sighed contently to show that he too was full, leaned back in his chair and turned his attention to purveying the elegant and impressive areas of adornment in the Oval Office.

"Very beautiful isn't it, Elvis?" President Nixon asked rhetorically, waving his right hand at all the historical photographs, ornaments and documents surrounding them.

"Very, very nice, Mr. President," Elvis agreed. Smiling, the 'King of Rock 'n Roll' added, "Very Presidential!"

President Nixon deliberately bobbled his head in full agreement. "Yes, Elvis, I agree. VERY Presidential."

Pat Nixon stood up and took a step towards Elvis and the President. "Richard, why don't you tell Elvis the REAL reason you have asked him to join you here at the White House for lunch?" The First Lady's face and body language turned very serious and stern as she stood before the two seated men and continued, "It's vitally important we get down to the business at hand with PROBABLY the only man alive who can pull off……" Pat cleared her throat, "essentially the ONLY man on Planet Earth who can pull off what we have in mind for the turbulent situation at hand…."

Pat spread her feet slightly in an even more demonstrative stance to continue her exhortation. "An unbelievably urgent matter that HAS to be dealt with." The look on the First Lady's face was deadly serious and changed her normally tranquil and stoic appearance that the world had come to recognize in her role as First Lady of the United States of America.

Elvis's forehead scrunched up into a dozen small horizontal lines as he shot perplexed glances between the First Lady and The President. Elvis was taken aback by the change in demeanor of President Nixon and the First Lady. Gone was the amiable couple who were enjoying a lunch of McDonalds cheeseburgers. In their place was a 'stone cold' man and woman with frowns and signs of worry over both faces.

President Nixon nodded his head toward his wife in appreciation. "You are correct Pat; this is a matter of monumental importance." He then turned in his chair toward Elvis, leaned forward with both elbows supported by the Oval Office's imposing desk. "Mr. Presley….er…. sorry…. ELVIS…the First Lady is correct!"

"Yes, Dick…..er, I mean Mr. President," Elvis snickered slightly as he addressed President Nixon, "I am all ears."

Without changing the seriousness etched across his face, President Nixon continued, "Elvis, we have a matter of National Security at hand that we feel can only be attended to by one man; 'The King of Rock 'n Roll, Mr. Elvis Aaron Presley !!"

Elvis's face turned serious, and he leaned back in his high-backed chair, with a pronounced inhale and exhale, taken aback by the solemnity and seriousness of Richard Milhous Nixon, the President of the United States of America.

CHAPTER FOUR

*(* Flashback to Monte Carlo)*

"Elvis ……are you serious …?!?! …. You mean to tell me that the President of the United States of America, Richard Milhous Nixon…who had a full culinary staff at his 'beck and call'…. ate a McDonalds cheeseburger for his lunch.?!?!?"

I, Dr. St. John quizzed the black haired one as I was in disbelief. Elvis batted his eyelids for a second and appeared in deep thought and the interruption in telling the story had derailed his train of thought for a moment.

After a few seconds of awkward silence, Katarina intervened, as it was obvious that Elvis was immersed in the story involving the past and deep in thought. "Elvis…" Katarina patted The King on his right knee then leaned over and kissed him on his cheek. Then the stunning Ukrainian 'model' with the luxurious locks twisted her torso slightly and whispered into Elvis' ear. "Dr. St. John has asked you a question, Baby…" continuing to pat Elvis on his knee.

Elvis's face evolved into a slow smile and his deep dark eyelashes batted repeatedly as the memories of the historic past flooded back into the recesses of his mind. "Oh, yes, Charlton Heston, yes, President Nixon and yes, the First Lady both enjoyed the delicious 'ordinary' treats from McDonalds, and ….OOPS….I meant Dr. Robert St. John…" Elvis proclaimed, enjoying teasing me about my resemblance to the star of ***The Ten Commandments.***

Not really knowing what to say about the 'compliment' of making me the personification of the Movie star…I shrugged my shoulders and said, "Thank you, Elvis."

The King smiled." Not a problem, Doctor. " It was apparent that Elvis had mentally removed himself from that day at the White House many years ago. He reached over and kissed Katarina lightly on her cheek. Then he turned directly to me saying, "Ok then, I will return to the story about the most pivotal day in my life."

(*Flashback ends. WH narrative resumes)

President Nixon stood up from behind the large oak desk, known as The Resolute Desk, a gift from The Queen of Great Britain and Ireland, so named because it was built from the timbers of the British vessel The HMS Resolute. The desk was situated strategically in the Oval office so as to place the President at the center of attention.

The President motioned for The First Lady to join him and he pulled up two chairs so that they could sit side by side with Elvis.

Instinctively Elvis sat straight up at attention as President Nixon pulled the two straight back chairs in a semicircular surrounding Elvis. The trio sat over the Presidential seal situated in the middle of the Oval office.

President Nixon cleared his voice. "Elvis, I am going to have to ask you to raise your right hand and swear on the Bible that what First Lady Pat Nixon is going to present to you, that what I am about to tell and confide in you, you will keep confidential until your death OR until the President of the United States of America releases you from this oath."

Elvis usually had a response to any kind of verbiage thrown his way, but this time, after the actions of President Nixon and the First Lady, he sat flabbergasted, in total silence.

Pat Nixon pulled out a small leather Bible from her purse and placed it gingerly on Elvis' knee. All he could do was shake his famous head up and down in agreement. Then President Nixon motioned for Elvis to place his left hand on the King James Version of the Bible, and instinctively and solemnly Elvis raised his right hand.

"Do you, Elvis Aaron Presley, solemnly swear to keep all that is said to you tonight, and explained to you here in the Oval Office by me, Richard Milhous Nixon, President of the United States of America in confidence and never divulge any of the following information to any person without the expressed written consent of the Commander-In-Chief of the United States of America, so help you God?"

Elvis dutifully sat in stunned silence in front of the President, his left hand on the Bible and his right hand held respectfully aloft in the stance of someone taking a solemn oath

After 4 to 5 seconds of silence, Pat Nixon looked directly at Elvis and asked intently, "Well, do you, Elvis?"

Elvis snapped back from his stunned silence and looked first at Pat Nixon then over at the President, his right hand still aloft and his deep dark eyes wide open. Stuttering and stammering Elvis repeated softly but intently, "I, Elvis Aaron Presley, swear to keep all that is explained and told and divulged to me today in total confidence and secrecy until otherwise expressly stated to me by the President of the United States of America."

The President interceded, "Elvis… do you solemnly swear this confidence to God?"

Elvis regained a bit of his composure and nodded affirmatively. "Yes, I solemnly swear this confidentiality so help me to the Lord my God."

From Elvis' expression it was still apparent that the King of Rock 'n Roll was shocked by the extreme level of seriousness his White House visit had turned into.

"Very well, Mr. Presley, Elvis Aaron Presley, NOT Vernon Presley…… you may take your left hand off the Bible and lower your right hand.

First Lady Pat Nixon reached over and took the Bible off his knee and placed the black leather sacrament back into her purse. She then turned to the President, serenely proclaiming, "I do believe that Elvis understands and appreciates the utmost seriousness of what we are going to tell him now."

President Nixon looked at The First Lady and nodded slowly in agreement. "And I believe Elvis will keep everything confidential for the rest of his life." As if to further punctuate his statement, he intensified the affirmative nodding, his face clearly showing the solemnity of the moment.

Elvis slowly lowered his hand and stared at President Nixon. "Mr. President, from my service in the United States Military, I had heard of very serious proceedings such as what I just went through."

Elvis spoke politely but firmly as he held his right hand up again, demonstrating his taking of the Presidential oath. "My commander in the Army underwent something similar while he was serving In Germany. Mister President, I have sworn to maintain my confidentiality the rest of my life, AND as I understand, the penalty if I violate my oath….. is DEATH!"   Elvis stared directly at President Nixon in the most solemn manner.

The First Lady and the President looked at each other intently. Then they directed their stares at Elvis and both enunciated slowly, fluently and simultaneously….. "Yes…..DEATH."

Elvis gazed at the President and First Lady intently. It seemed as if a 'lifetime' had passed as Elvis torqued over and over in his brain the in-credible happenings so far of that day at The White House. Elvis' life seemed to 'flash in front of his eyes' as he was in 'shock and awe.' Then Elvis blurted out, "OK" shaking his jet-black mane back and forth wildly. "I PROMISE I will keep silent about what is happening today and what is being told and revealed to me here at The White House for the rest of my life." He continued to nod even more vigorously …." and I understand it will mean the 'death of me' if I divulge any of the following that is disclosed to me today."

Elvis took a strong crossed-arms stance and continued, "President Nixon, I swear to you that I will NOT tell anyone what you are about to reveal to me."

He looked first at President Nixon then the First Lady. He sighed intently, continuing to stand with his arms crossed over his chest, "So, where do we begin?" Elvis inquired, a quizzical look painted over his world-famous visage.

"Yes," President Nixon said in agreement. Where DO we begin...?" he asked tentatively, glancing hopefully at The First Lady for her help starting this incredibly important conversation.

CHAPTER FIVE

Dr. Robert St. John sat up. "Elvis Aaron Presley! Why didn't you tell me all this years and years ago!?! "

Elvis was taken aback by the good doctor's demeanor. The King grimaced slightly and glanced over at Katarina. Katarina looked back at Elvis, shrugged her shoulders and declared forcefully, "It's up to you Elvis, baby!"

Elvis recuperated enough to say, "Dr. St. John, I could not tell you years ago because I was under a solemn oath with the President of the United States of America and had a couple of huge, herculean tasks that were assigned to me that absolutely had to be completed for the sake of our mother country, the United States of America!"

"OK, OK!" Dr. St. John slapped his hands together. "I understand that!" The 'Charlton Heston look-alike' shot a glance at Katarina and shrugged, asking her somewhat offhandedly, "So what's different now, love?"

Katarina grinned precociously, tapped her chest authoritatively with her finger, and quipped, "*I* am new and different… and the best!"

Elvis, hearing Katarina's response, smiled wryly at her and said, "Yes baby, you ARE the best!" Elvis sprang up exuberantly from his seat. "Hold on, Dr St John!" He strode over to the Monte Carlo villa's wall and took a plaque off of its hook. He then turned and held it out to Dr. St. John with both hands extended in a triumphant manner. "The Congressional and Presidential Medal of Freedom!" Elvis smiled broadly, his pride very apparent. He then reached behind the celebrated plaque and pulled out a paper document that had been attached to the back. He whipped the starched letter around in the air as if it was a winning lottery ticket. "…and this letter from President Ronald Reagan allows and permits me to fully discuss my complete accomplishment with you, Dr. St. John. "Do you wish me to read it out loud to you?" Elvis announced as he continually brandished the letter with the US Presidential Seal adorning the top.

Dr. St. John held up his right hand in a polite refusal and replied, NO need, Elvis, but feel free to summarize it to me."

Elvis nodded in agreement. "Okie dokie then!" Clearing his throat for effect and continuing to hold the Presidentially Sealed paper high above his head for Dr. St John to see, he stood up straighter and gushed, "In summation……..this official document"… Elvis continued to exhibit the letter from Presidents Reagan and Clinton, waving it ever closer to Dr. St. John's eyes, "…..declares in official Presidential verbiage that to the extent I sacrificed my life, my family and of course my fantastically wonderful singing/acting career in service of my country, the United States of America, we hereby…therefore, designate and award this medal…etc., etc.." He abruptly stopped, chuckling at himself for his feigning of ceremonial pomposity, finishing with a faux formal bow from the waist.

Katarina looked up at Elvis and smiled the most bodacious grin of affection that anyone could imagine. She adored it when he showed his humor.

Dr. St. John sat in Elvis' beautiful seaside villa in Monte Carlo in admiration and stunned silence, not really knowing how to respond.

"So, Dr. St. John, I could not tell you so much when you were chasing me around the world. Remember, I did not expect anyone to chase me around the world like you did!" Elvis rolled his dark eyes expressively in disbelief. "You showed up everywhere I moved to!"

Elvis' statement snapped Dr. St. John back to reality and back to verbal functionality. "Thank you; thank you very much…" Dr. St. John replied, beaming broadly. Then he continued, deciding to explain his extraordinary 'gypsy' trek around the world in pursuit of the King of Rock 'n Roll. "Well, as you may remember Elvis, it was not my idea to go dig up your grave at Graceland only to discover that your resting place was empty!"

Elvis held up his hand in recognition of the veracity of what Dr. St. John was espousing… "I understand," Elvis sighed…" BUT…. I have given you the full scenario today of WHY I could not give you more information than what I did."

Dr. St. John sighed, "Elvis Aaron Presley, you have given me a snapshot of the reasons you left your life…"

Katarina looked over at Dr. St. John, her flowing brown hair dancing in the Mediterranean breeze as she proclaimed in her tinged Ukrainian English… "So, do you want Elvis to tell you the WHOLE STORY NOW?" The Eastern European beauty narrowed her gaze and tilted her head as she eagerly anticipated Dr. St. John's answer. He took a deep sigh in response to her quizzical look. "Of course, I do," he spat out toward both Elvis and Katarina.

"Thank you…… thank you very much!" Katarina smiled and responded in her best broken English, mimicking her boyfriend's traditional salutation.

Elvis could not help but to snicker softly at Katarina's response. He jumped up to his feet, swiveled his hips and slapped his hands together. "Ok, Dr. St. John, I will pick up the story right where all this phenomenal incredible, unbelievable saga began!!" Elvis swiveled his hips some more in typical Elvis fashion…..and literally sang out in his wonderfully unmistakable, beautiful, melodic, world-famous Elvis voice….(to the tune of 'Mine Eyes Have Seen The Glory'): *"When I met with Pat and Richard Nixon at the…… White House…"*

Elvis laughed loudly at his own antics and looked over at the beautiful Katarina, smiled and winked, and then smiled back at Dr St. John.

CHAPTER SIX

"Ok then, I am going to tell the story that until today only Presidents of the United States of America have known." Elvis quit his swiveling and singing , and his countenance suddenly turned extremely solemn.

Katarina stepped forward, tilted her lovely face, and with a bewildered and pleading look in her eyes, plaintively said, "Elvis baby, I thought I knew *everything...* "

Elvis stepped forward and slowly and deliberately extended his right index finger and placed it gingerly over Katarina's bountiful lips. "Shhhhh".... He lowly whispered, calling her by her pet Elvis name. "Kitty Kat, you know that you basically do know everything, but...let me tell you and Dr. St. John the FULL story in chronological order so that he understands everything too."

Katarina gently pulled Elvis's silencing finger away from her mouth. Then, in her decidedly European flavored and fragmented English, said,   "…chrono……   what   ….who ……when…order ??"

Elvis giggled…."Baby Kitty Kat, I am going to tell you MY story from start to finish exactly how things happened."

"Ok Elvis….." Katarina purred…."go ahead and tell the story that only the Presidents of the United States of America know,…" exclaiming in a way that made it clear she knew she was indeed included in special company.

Elvis smiled at the Ukrainian and replied "Katarina, you can be so buoyant and …."

Katarina interrupted…. "Elvis, not a lecture right now. I am like Dr. St. John; I also want to hear the whole story….. I must admit I am very very intrigued !!"

Elvis reacted, "Baby Kitty Kat, you know that you know the whole story !!"

Katarina purred….."I know I do, baby… I just want to hear you tell it all out loud exactly the way it happened. I want to hear you tell it to a third party…." Katarina pointed to Dr. St John.." Please tell the story to Dr. St. John and I will sit here and be an interested onlooker, an observer only…"

Elvis nodded his head up and down after understanding and appreciating Katarina's quiet dissertation on hearing the story told out loud to another person.

All three took their respective places, Elvis and Katarina on the plush sofa and Dr. St .John on the adjacent large chair. Suddenly Elvis jumped up from his place by Katarina, swiveled his hips a bit, "I am so used to standing when….performing for an audience…."

Both Katarina and Dr. St .John nodded their heads in agreement with Elvis' demonstration.

"Ok," Elvis began, "You can understand how taken aback I was when President Nixon and the First Lady, Pat Nixon hit me 'out of the blue' about serving our country as they did. I had served in the military but what they were going to ask me to do was so C-R-A-Z-Y! I must admit I had to put my head in both my hands and close my eyes to digest all of it."

Elvis stood in front of his audience of two and placed his head in both hands and simply shook it as if to recreate that moment from the past. Katarina and Dr. St. John glanced at each other in surprise and showed some quiet concern at Elvis standing in front of them demonstrating such dramatic emotions precipitated from that event. It was apparent from Elvis' actions that all of this was still somewhat of a burden to him even after all the time that had passed.

"BABY!" Katarina exclaimed aloud as she elevated herself from her seat on the sofa.

Elvis jerked a bit in response to Katarina, removing his head from his hands, regaining his composure. Elvis smiled slyly and pointed his right index finger at her. "Sit down baby, I am fine."

Katarina realized this was a serious reaction from Elvis, one that she had not really seen before, and immediately retook her seat. She relaxed and slumped a bit back into her place on the plush purple futon.

"First," Elvis swept his pointed right index finger at both of his seated audience members,

"I'm going to ask that you two promise me that you will not tell ANYONE or speak of what I am going to divulge to you for…" Elvis glanced up at the ceiling of the Monte Carlo villa deep in thought… then declared…"5 years!" Elvis continued to shake his pointed right index finger at his 2 audience members in a serious manner which indicated he demanded a response. Dr. St. John and Katarina both nodded in acquiescence and simultaneously declared, "Agreed."

(Meanwhile, back at the White House…)

CHAPTER SEVEN

"We, our country, the USA has a problem, Elvis" President Nixon declared. The President arose from behind his desk in the Oval Office and strode over to where Elvis sat on the sofa next to First Lady Pat Nixon. The leader of the free world stood directly in front of Elvis and continued, "Elvis, do you have any idea why I called you here to the White House, and that I am going to ask you to help confront a perilous situation?"

Elvis sat flabbergasted and shook his head 'no,' revealing that The King of Rock 'n Roll did not have a clue.

The President sat back down at his desk, rested his left elbow on the desk, then his chin on his hand before continuing, "Elvis, it's because you served our military in Germany and had an exemplary record."

Elvis looked over at President Nixon, began to nod his head in acknowledgement and said, "OK, Mr. President, I guess I can understand."

"Elvis, when we defeated Adolf Hitler, Germany and Japan and ended the Second World War, the USA gained a lot of authority, support and power."

Elvis nodded his head in concurrence. "Yes, Mr. President, I agree the USA did gain lots of power and authority when we defeated Hitler, Germany and Japan."

President Nixon got up from the desk, took one step toward the seated Elvis and raised his right hand and stated emphatically "But , with that monumental success and victory we created some powerful enemies."

Elvis sat solemnly and nodded his head again in agreement. "Yes Mr. President, we did."

President Nixon took a deep breath and sighed as he continued, "In particular, the Soviet Union !"

Again Elvis signified his agreement. "Yes, Sir, Mr. President, I totally agree. The main reason I was stationed in Germany was due to the power and presence of the Soviet Union."

The President looked directly and deeply into Elvis' eyes. "That is absolutely correct, Elvis"

Elvis nodded again and reiterated, "possibly the number one main reason I was stationed in Germany was the Soviet Bloc…"

First Lady Pat Nixon assented and pitched in, "Reason #1." She continued, "and that is one of the main reasons you are here Elvis….just as the President has stated, AND Elvis…you understand the power and the threat of Russia and the Soviet Union because you were in Germany and saw this first hand."

Then President Nixon cleared his throat and in a calm tone, said, "Now, bear with us just a bit Elvis, and be patient, while we tell you a story that you do not know, but one that it is imperative for you to hear to understand our predicament."

Mrs. Nixon interrupted, "Elvis, absolutely no one outside of the White House and Intelligence Community knows this story. NO ONE." The First Lady continued, "…and this is the main reason you CAN NOT divulge this story to anyone."

Elvis' wide eyes revealed his interest and intrigue, and he gazed first at President Nixon and then at the First Lady in a manner that tacitly stated…" OK, I am listening!"

"Elvis, the First Lady is 100% absolutely positively correct. Only a handful of people on Planet Earth know this story and ALL OF THEM…. everyone who knows… has taken an oath not to divulge the story. They are allowed to say nothing!"

Elvis again indicated his understanding and agreement. "Absolutely correct, President Nixon, I will not talk to anyone about what I hear today in the Oval Office…...no one!"

The First Lady interjected, "Be patient with the long story and dialogue Elvis, because after you hear the entire narrative, my husband, the President of these United States, will be asking you to perform an unbelievably great service for your country."

Elvis smiled and nodded his head "President and First Lady, I am always glad to be of service to my country."

President Nixon held up both his hands in a defensive gesture and admonished, "Wait, Elvis." He moved his head slightly side to side in an incredulous manner. "Wait until you hear this story….AND…what I as President of the United States will ask you to do before you agree to these huge sacrifices for your country…and…the World."

Elvis stared at an empty space between President Nixon and the First Lady, sat quietly for a moment before slowly lifting his head slightly to bring them both into his direct line of sight. Then, in a firm but respectful tone, said, "I understand."

"Ok, good, then we are set," Nixon stated as he backed up and sat down on the edge of the desk. He settled on the desk, where he faced Elvis and Pat. The President turned towards his wife and asked politely and in subdued manner, "Pat, do you mind getting us all a Coca-Cola as this will take a while"

"Not a problem, Mr. President." Pat smiled broadly as she politely referred to her husband deferentially as 'President'. Then the First Lady stared at Elvis expectantly.

Elvis requested, "May I have my Coke with ice, please?"

Mrs. Nixon walked to one side of the Oval office, opened a cabinet and poured three iced Coca-Colas. As The First Lady handed out the liquid refreshments, the President declared from his sitting space on his desk, "Ok then, let's get started."

CHAPTER EIGHT

President Nixon took a drink of Coca-Cola, sighed ……then sat the glass down on the desk. He then crossed his arms across his chest and looked Elvis directly in the eye. "Elvis did you know that Adolph Hitler and Eva Braun had a child together? Hearing no immediate response, President Nixon twisted his head slightly to ask again, "Elvis, did you know Adolf Hitler and Eva Braun had a child together?

Elvis took a sip from his Coca-Cola and replied, "No Sir, I did not ."

The President reciprocated Elvis' actions and took a sip out of his Coca-Cola and President Nixon retorted, "Not many people on Planet Earth know this little-known fact ,but it is true." Adolf Hitler's and Eva Braun's offspring, a boy, was named Ivan and he was born in 1940."

Elvis nodded his head in acknowledgment and replied "That's an amazing bit of information, President Nixon. I had no idea that Adolf Hitler and Eva Braun had a son!"

Elvis contorted his face in a questioning gaze and asked President Nixon "So, what does this have to do with me?" He glanced over at the First Lady and scratched his head in a non-understanding gesture.

The First Lady jumped up and exclaimed, "Dick, let me at least explain Ivan Hitler's childhood!" ..." Please! Let me! Pat Nixon implored of her husband.

President Nixon looked directly at his wife then back at Elvis. To emphasize this action, he repeated it, looking first at Pat and then directly back at Elvis. "The childhood of Ivan Hitler is imperative to understanding why you, Elvis Aaron Presley, are here today, and why you were sworn to secrecy by the President of the United States of America."

"REALLY!" Elvis gushed. The King of Rock 'n Roll averted his gaze from the President and fixated on the First Lady." Now I can't wait to hear this story!" Elvis bellowed, taking another drink of Coke, then swirling the cubes around in the glass, clanging them against the periphery in excitement.

"OK Pat, give Elvis the background of Adolf Hitler's son, Ivan, then I will explain what Ivan Hitler has to do with Elvis being here today and "……President Nixon paused, taking another sip of Coca Cola……"What Elvis Aaron Presley can do for the USA…...and the W O R L D !!!"

The First Lady walked over to her husband, The President. She extended her right hand and Richard lovingly and dutifully took it. Pat gingerly guided him to a position on the sofa next to Elvis. Then she took center stage right in front of the two gentlemen on the Presidential Seal rug. Pat began to nervously pace back and forth in front of Elvis and her husband. She suddenly stopped, directly in the middle of the Presidential Seal, took a defiant stance there and stated emphatically, "It will take a woman's point of view to explain the events surrounding Ivan Hitler, particularly his youth, and how this is so fundamentally relevant to you, Elvis."

"Thank you, thank you very much!" Elvis responded with his signature courtesy, which automatically elicited smiles from both the First Lady and President Nixon.

CHAPTER NINE

"As a mother, I would hardly or probably not understand the trauma of having a child during such a horrifying period of time such as World War II." Pat proclaimed as she started to pace back and forth in front of the spellbound audience of two. With her head held somewhat down, she continued. "As you know, Elvis, at the beginning of World War II, Germany held the upper hand over Great Britain, France and the rest of Europe"

President Nixon nodded his head in agreement with his wife.

"England held out and was the 'thorn' in Germany and Hitler's 'side'. This early point of WW II was when Ivan was propagated and born." Pat cleared her throat and emitted a slight sigh, then continued. "Ivan's early childhood was when the conflict began to morph and began to go the Allies' way, and things started going bad for Hitler and Germany."

*(*Flashback to Hitler/Braun home c. late '40s)*

"Mommie, I don't want to leave and go live with Aunt Hilda in Ukraine or Russia or… wherever!" Ivan Hitler screamed as his blonde haired Aunt Hilda attempted to pull young Ivan out of Mother Eva Braun's grasp. Streams of hot salty tears flowed down Eva's face as she relinquished control of her only child, Ivan.

Adolf Hitler, Ivan's father, walked reluctantly into the emotionally morass unfolding in the Hitler's home in Berlin.

"Ivan Hitler, quit your crying and let your Aunt Hilda take you as you have been ordered to do by your Mother!" Adolf Hitler walked up and snatched his screaming son Ivan from Eva's arms and briskly handed the sobbing trembling youngster to the awaiting arms of Hilda.

(Meanwhile, back at the White House…)

Elvis, his face now emanating shock and amazement, held up his hand and interrupted Mrs. Nixon's intriguing tale. "Missus First Lady…… is all of this true?"

Pat Nixon took a determined stance with her feet and crossed her arms across her chest and shook her head up and down in the affirmative. "Yes Elvis, every word of this tale is true !"

President Nixon interrupted, "We think it is vitally important to give you a verbal history of some very important and unknown happenings in the past to give you an understanding of what is happening and why we need to get you involved, Elvis!"

Elvis nodded his head in understanding. "Don't misunderstand, I am listening. It's just that I am in shock about some of this revelation about Ivan."

The President repeated, "The First Lady will get to the most important information about this story shortly, BUT, we believe that Pat's giving this background information to you is very, very important to understanding the task at hand. "

After a momentary pause Elvis looked at President Nixon "OK, agreed" Elvis then looked at Pat Nixon "OK, Ms. First Lady, sorry about the interruption. I will be silent and listen, please proceed with this intriguing story."

"It's Pat, Elvis…please call me Pat!" The First lady looked at the King of Rock 'n Roll with appreciation, reminding him again that he was among friends now, and terms of familiarity were totally acceptable.

"Then Pat it is…!" Elvis gushed, smiling broadly at the First Lady.

Pat Nixon side took a deep breath and then resumed the story. "I'm going to take a little time now to flesh out the rest of the story about the childhood of Ivan Hitler. So, Ivan was carried off to another locale at orders of his dad, Adolf Hitler, but mostly at discretion of his mother, Eva Braun. No matter how well the war seemed to be going, Eva was not assuaged. She knew she felt down deep that if the war turned out bad, little Ivan, with his Hitler temper, would still survive with his cousin, Katarina Khrushchev."

"Oh my God, Katarina!!! Is this YOU they're talking about!?" Dr. St. John twirled around and looked directly at Elvis' woman Katarina.

Katrina smiled and responded, "Elvis will tell you the rest of the story about President and

Mrs. Nixon. She then held her hands palms up in a 'you shall see' gesture while pointing to Elvis, declaring "That will have to wait. You tell the rest of the story, Elvis ."

Dr. St .John shook his head in disbelief as this tale was becoming crazier and crazier and crazier with each twist and turn in the chain of events that were unfolding. Dr. St. John looked at Elvis and threw up his hands. "Sorry I interrupted," he said apologetically, pointing at Katarina, "but hey, I just had to know if this is the Katarina that the story is alluding to. "Please go on Elvis, because NOW I can't wait to hear the rest of the tale in its entirety !"

Elvis declared, "OK....back to the White House. We will resume at the point where Mrs. Nixon was explaining why Ivan was taken away by.... some young lady.... named Katarina!"

"It appears Eva Braun and the Khrushchev family wanted Ivan Hitler to go to the Ukraine; anywhere away from Berlin." Eva felt things were going to turn out wrong. Adolf was so busy with all of the military operations that were going on at that time against the Allies, he did not say much when Eva stated she wanted Ivan to go live with her cousins, the Khrushchevs. Hitler did not know where Eva's family was from, and with him being so preoccupied with everything, he did not care. He simply wanted his son, Ivan safe, and as Ivan wanted Eva's attention all of the time, it was best for Eva to arrange everything...

Hilda continued to pull little Ivan from Eva's arms as he continued to resist. Eva declared, "you will see Mama soon, Ivan." Tears began to stream down Eva's cheeks. "Hilda's going to take you to Aunt Katarina's farm a for a nice vacation." Eva kept swiping tears that were pouring down her face as Hilda continued to tug at Ivan. Finally, Hilda gathered Ivan and began to walk with her precious package out of the room.

Eva Braun yelled after her departing son "Ivan, you will love your cousin Katarina and living in Ukraine with your relatives, the Khrushchevs. "Nikita Khrushchev in particular will love you, young man." Ivan was screaming at the top of his lungs as Eva continued to wipe tears from her eyes , trying to comfort him with her words.

Ivan did not respond as he had quit his outburst and had buried himself into the firm grasp of his new caretaker, his nursemaid, Hilda. The young nursemaid carried her distraught package out of the Berlin apartment and loaded him into an awaiting vehicle. which would transport Ivan Hitler to what Eva Braun hoped would be security and safety.

Elvis held up his hand as if he were in the 3rd grade wanting permission to ask a question. "Mrs. Nixon , what in the world does all of this about the child Ivan Hitler have to do with me?"

President Nixon held his hand up in a 'don't answer' signal to his wife. After looking at his wife reassuringly, President Nixon rotated toward Elvis. "Elvis, I am going to ask you to do me a favor. Please do something for me."

Elvis nodded his head in agreement, but with a scowl of puzzlement scrawled over his face.

"Be patient, Elvis, because…. as President of the United States I am going to ask you in a few minutes to do something so unbelievable and so extraordinary. In order for you to understand the full rationale and reasoning behind this most extraordinary request, please, please be patient as The First Lady goes through the total dissertation and explanation of what has happened, what might happen, how we got here, and what in the world we are going to do to try to avoid the loss or destruction of Planet Earth."

With that long explanation by President Nixon, Elvis shyly dropped his hand back to his side and nodded in recognition of the apparent severity of the pending dilemma and the reason Mrs. Nixon had to explain in such exacting detail about what events and occurrences had apparently precipitated this gargantuan problem.

Pat asked softly and politely, "Elvis, is it OK if I continue with the story now?"

'Yes, of course, Pat" Elvis responded just as politely. I will be patient."

The First Lady took a quick gulp of Coca-Cola and took a deep, deep breath and resumed the story where she had left off. "Hilda struggled to quiet and placate the young Ivan Hitler as they made their away from the villa and Ivan's parents.

Elvis held up his right hand again in 3rd grade fashion. This time Pat sighed in slight annoyance at the interruption and asked, "What now, Elvis?" clanking her Coca-Cola down on the desk.

"I was wondering, with Germany and Russia basically at War, how could Hilda take Ivan to the Ukraine?"

"OK Elvis, a GREAT question" Pat picked up her glass and took a deep gulp, then continued, "Eva Braun had strong Ukrainian AND German connections which helped her facilitate the transfer of her ONLY son to her family because of these connections. It's complicated!"

The serious-minded look on Elvis' face showed an understanding and recognition of the complexity of the situation, "Well, because I was stationed in Germany for two years, I understand the animosity between Germany and Russia, I know how complex it is.... but... I will shut up and listen."

Pat shook her head affirmatively, picked up her drink again, and continued her explanation of events surrounding the transference of Hitler's son to a safe hiding place in the Ukraine during the height of the chaos precipitated by the 2nd World War.

Between sobs, Ivan looked up and grabbed Hilda's long blonde hair and buried his tortured face into her long golden locks. Nursemaid Hilda tightly held the 'sobbing load' and headed to in the back seat of the silver Mercedes.

As Hilda settled into the vehicle, she carefully placed her terrified protégé who had been in her tutelage for 2 years in place beside her. She carefully took Ivan's grasping hands and pulled them away from her tangled hair. Then the blonde nursemaid adjusted herself and situated Ivan more carefully in the seat as close to her as she could, and clutched him in a comforting and reassuring manner. Turning to the driver, she declared, "Let's make way while we have morning light," and waved her free hand to mean, 'let's go.'

The driver, who was called Claude, asked, "Are we still headed by the remote back way to our destination in the Ukraine?" He then looked over his right shoulder and peered directly at Hilda after his question to make sure that he understood his instructions.

"Yes, we are, Claude…it is Claude, isn't it?"

The driver nodded and smiled, "Correct….it is Claude"

"Yes, Claude we will in fact have to take the unmarked back road as we travel East. Please take us as far as you can in this vehicle on the Autobahn."

Ivan, Hilda and Claude the driver turned from the Hitler Berlin villa in calmness and drove East away from Ivan's beloved mother and father so the youngster could start a new life in relative safety in Ukraine.

CHAPTER TEN

First Lady Pat Nixon sat her Coca-Cola glass down and poured herself another drink of the carbonated confection. "Sorry guys, my mouth got dry," she apologized, taking another sip.

President Nixon interrupted, "Elvis, Pat is going thru this long convoluted explanation for you because, and you have to trust me on this, it is vital to your understanding of this very complex situation our country faces, and the great patriotic favor that I, as President, am asking of you.

Elvis glanced first at President Nixon and then at the First Lady, signaled agreement with a nod and acknowledged, "I truly understand and appreciate the intriguing narrative ….the First Lady…er…. I mean Pat, is relaying to me." Elvis continued to direct his gaze between the First Lady and the President.

"Ok then, "Pat Nixon responded as she put down the clear glass she had just emptied. Then slapping her hands together symbolizing she was ready to restart her discourse, "Elvis, let me complete the story of Ivan Hitler's youth. Then I will move aside and allow the President to take up the story of why you are here."

Elvis smiled and simply nodded his head up and down in accord. "Thank you, First Lady…err …. Pat. Please continue whenever you are ready finish the tale about the youth of Ivan Hitler. I must admit my interest has been piqued."

Pat Nixon allowed a slow smile then glanced at her husband, President of the USA and then back to Elvis.

"OK then. Eventually Ivan calmed down in Hilda's reassuring and comforting embrace." The First Lady directed her story straight at Elvis. Adding details, she said, "Claude, the driver, a hulking, somewhat grotesque man, drove the Autobahn in the direction of East Germany and towards the Ukraine."

Unknown to German and certainly to American Intelligence, there was an old connection between Eva Braun and the old aristocratic Russian family, the Khrushchevs. This old-line Russian family was essentially neutral, à la the Mountain

Island nation of Switzerland. The Khrushchevs were landowners in both Ukraine and Moscow.

Eva Braun was descended on her mother's side distantly to the Khrushchev family tree. Eva knew that with her abstract family branch of the Khrushchevs, and given their traveling distance from Moscow, their neutrality and land holdings would offer a very safe haven for her only son, Ivan.

This was a calculated gamble by Eva Braun, but she decided that 'discretion is the better part of valor.' She was going to place little Ivan in the loyal and competent hands of her mother's family lineage and she thought this would assure Ivan's safety. Eva's close contacts inside the German female hierarchy had 'whispered' to Eva that since America had joined the Allies after Pearl Harbor, that it was possible Germany's march across Europe might be repelled en masse. Regardless, Eva felt that placing Ivan in the relative safety of Grandmother Khrushchev's isolated Ukrainian estate near Kiev was the prudent and wise thing to do, considering the uncertainty of the war's out-come, AND if her internal instincts were proven wrong, and Germany prevailed at the end of the war, Eva could then go and claim her prized only offspring, Ivan Hitler.

Claude drove steadfastly out the Autobahn. Then abruptly the sizeable driver pointed to a side road. "Miss Hilda, unfortunately we are going to have to take that harsh road up ahead." Claude torqued his macabre face to convey his feelings of dread in the tortuous path they must follow. "Young lady, we will have to switch to a 4-wheel drive vehicle as we must traverse the old back way over farmland and prairie and woods to Kiev."

Hilda nodded to signify her understanding, the now exhausted Ivan snug and tight to her chest, quickly falling asleep. Claude slowly pulled the Mercedes off the Autobahn onto the exit way he had pointed out to Hilda. A military officer stepped out from behind a hedge row and waved for the driver of the vehicle to come to a stop. Claude did so, and then exited the Mercedes. He saluted the officer and handed him a folded paper. The officer unfolded the document and glanced briefly through it. After scrutinizing the paper instrument Claude had handed him, the officer's posture took an immediate change from relaxation to attention. Following a brief discussion between the two men, the officer turned and pointed to a small grass trail that traversed over the hill and Hilda heard Claude say, "Thank you, officer."

Claude returned to the Mercedes and turned in the seat to face Hilda. "Miss, we are headed over that hill and will change vehicles there."

Claude glanced at the still slumbering Ivan situated in Hilda's comforting arms and flashed a gratuitous smile. He then returned his attention to directing their vehicle over the grassy knoll. A small wooden hut and supply post was situated over the small hill that could be discerned when the Mercedes topped the apex. Another German, clad in military attire, stood at attention as the vehicle approached him and the outpost he manned.

Claude pulled adjacent to the building, hopped out of the Mercedes and submitted the official letter to the officer, holding the document within mere inches of the gentleman's face. Quickly assuaging the information, the German officer bowed his head in understanding and strode around the small building and immediately returned in a German military vehicle. The officer stepped out and took Claude by the elbow and showed him a map with detailed instructions on how to drive in the non-military zone off-road paths so they could arrive safely and unnoticed to their destination and hiding place outside of Kiev, Ukraine.

Claude nodded his head in agreement and understanding after the officer laid out in explicit detail how to follow the written guidelines on the terrain map to Kiev, then walked around to the back door and opened the door for Hilda and Ivan. The nursemaid stepped out, her long blonde hair dangling over young Ivan, still semi-comatose from exhaustion. The giant driver directed her to the passenger compartment of the 4-wheel drive all-terrain vehicle. "I've never ridden in a military car like this," Hilda gushed. "Read about them, but never even seen one." The German officer overheard the blonde woman's statement. "Nurse, these vehicles are new!" obviously proud that his unit had been assigned such a prestigious new machine.

Claude saluted the officer, who returned the salute. Hilda loaded her still sleeping baby human cargo into the passenger side with her.

Claude turned the vehicle on and then slowly but surely began to direct the vehicle laden with the trio through the backwoods of Germany and on toward their manifest destiny in Kiev.

The back pathway to Kiev was rough and tortuous, but Claude was diligent in trying to guide the 4-wheel drive motor vehicle and his two passengers away from any military conflict. It seemed at times that Claude was constantly going up a precariously steep boulevard so remote was the passageway leading from Germany to the Ukraine.

An hour into the grueling trip, Ivan grunted and whirled up from his exhausted slumber. The youngster looked up into the deep blue eyes of Hilda and flashed a calming smile at his familiar caretaker. Then he glanced at the intimidating facial features of Claude, screamed at the top of his lungs and grabbed Hilda tightly and clung onto his protective mentor in horror. But so fatigued emotionally was the youngster that his brown eyes rolled back in his head and he collapsed back into a passed-out state on Hilda's lap. Claude reacted calmly to the young Ivan's hysterical reaction to Claude's outlandish physical appearance, and the leviathan driving the 4-wheeler simply smiled and shook his head in incredulity.

Claude conscientiously continued his push in the unmarked 4-wheeled drive vehicle carrying his precious cargo through the rough path overgrown with vegetation and other ecological obstructions. The rough-drawn map that was given to Claude was remarkable in that the trail that he followed was not clearly demarcated except by three notches carved on western aspect of landmark trees lining the way. Most of the skimpy trail was almost overgrown with small brush, scrub and saplings, but Claude remained confident that he was making the correct navigational decisions based on the 'shepherding' three notches etched in trees along the way.

Hilda held the slumbering and sleep-talking Ivan tightly as the wildly harsh terrain was at times unbelievably torturous. Ivan would talk incessantly to illusory Adolph and then to Eva as he bounced up and down on Hilda's lap. Claude glanced back in the passengers' compartment and directed, "You relax and sleep if you can. We have a long bouncy way to go yet."

Ivan reacted to Claude's voice and screamed as he awakened, "Where is my Mom and my Dad? then deciding to be more exact…."Where is Adolf and Eva….?" Ivan quizzed, as he looked around at the rugged terrain that surrounded them in their vehicle. Then the youngster looked up at his burly chauffer, Claude, and then at his nursemaid, Hilda. Apparently still half asleep and in incredulity that he had been shipped off by his beloved parents, Adolf and Eva, Ivan twisted his head right and left in a desperate attempt to assess and understand his surroundings.

Hilda reached and gathered Ivan back into her warming embrace and patted her inquisitive charge lovingly on his tousled hair covered head. "Ivan, your Mom and Dad, Adolf and Eva could not accompany us on our trip." Still patting Ivan on the top of the head in a reassuring and very German manner, "you are here with me, who you know very well, and our strong chauffer, Claude."

In realization of his predicament, Ivan snorted, squirmed back into his seat, crossed his petite arms defensively over his chest, showing in a very nonverbal display his disgust that he could not be with his mother and father.

Hilda continued to stroke her young protégé on his head in a nurturing and reassuring manner. "Ivan, dear, everything will be OK," Hilda cooed soothingly, leaned forward and smiled directly to Ivan's face.

Claude glanced back over the front seat at Ivan and Hilda. "The road has been challenging and may get even more difficult," Claude grimaced and torqued his repulsive face to indicate the challenge that might lie ahead. "BUT," he commanded, "I will get us through to our destination no matter how monumental the hurdles and difficulties!"

He continued his reassurance, "My lad and lass, when we go thru Poland… which of course Germany now commands… the road gets rougher; then we will push toward Kiev!! Claude asserted his belief in himself by demonstrably rocking his head in a positive back and forth fashion, as he promised safe arrival at their destination regardless of the difficulties that might face them.

CHAPTER ELEVEN

"Elvis, do you need me to take a break? This is a very lengthy story about Ivan Hitler, BUT it is imperative you know Ivan Hitler's total overall history." Pat Nixon had interrupted her dissertation just long enough to ask her Oval office guest a question pertaining to his personal comfort.

Elvis looked up quickly from his Coca-Cola glass, raising his hand and shaking his head ever so slightly to tacitly signal to The First Lady that he was fine, and for her to continue.

Pat sighed "Well, indeed this is a very pro-longed narrative, Elvis. but again, and I repeat, it is vitally crucial that I convey to you the Ivan Hitler history in such a detailed manner."

"Pat, I am here attentively listening to every detail, and I understand," Elvis said as he threw his arms out into the air and squirmed deep into the luxurious Oval Office couch so as to achieve more comfort while sitting and absorbing every word of this story."

"OK then, GREAT!" Pat responded as she smiled and shook her empty glass at her husband, President Nixon, nodding her head at the large quart Coca-Cola bottle on the desk, signifying she needed a refill to quench her thirst.

Dutifully, the President of the United States, arguably the most powerful man on Planet Earth, walked over and the large bottle filled with the brown liquid confection and refilled his wife's glass. Then reflexively, President Nixon shuffled across the room, imitating a "certain performer' (with the full hopes of endearing himself to the King of Rock 'n Roll), took the large bottle over to Elvis, and with a cheesy grin, refilled his glass. They both laughed at this impromptu informality.

"Thank you, thank you very much!" Elvis replied and watched as The President plopped down on the comfortable sofa. The President lifted and waved his right hand in a 'carry on' fashion and motioned for Pat to continue her story. Mrs. Nixon took a swift swig of her drink, clanking the ice cubes against the inner part of her Waterford Crystal glass to accentuate her actions, and then continued unpacking the details of the story she was telling.

CHAPTER TWELVE

"So," Mrs. Nixon hastily summarized, "Hilda looked over the front seat at Claude and shrugged her shoulders, we understand, and 'as she patted her protégé' Ivan's knee reassuringly again, AND..." Claude sighed, looking up in the rear view mirror at Hilda and gave a worried look..." then tensely whispered, "We have not encountered any Military convoys..."

"I know." Hilda looked up into the mirror. "And Claude, we don't want to run into any tanks or other artillery, or the like."

Claude smiled and shook his head up and down reassuringly and in agreement. Then the huge man looked back at the cargo, the 6-year-old offspring of Adolf Hitler and Eva Braun had nodded off asleep again. Claude patted his own bald head and after viewing the slumbering Ivan, mouthed "good" in a 'non-vocal verbalization' to show his appreciation of Hilda's difficult chore that lay ahead.

"Hilda, we are going south of Warsaw, so hopefully we won't be bothered one bit during the trip to Kiev." Claude's pronouncement made Hilda smile. Ivan aroused a bit out of his sleep, reached over and instinctively clasped Hilda's hand in reassurance. Then Ivan's head began to slowly nod back and forth and he slipped back into sleep from exhaustion and stress.

"Stop!" A sharp command rang out as two uniformed Russian officers jumped out of the brushy undergrowth onto the wilderness trail. Claude slammed on the brakes and the 4 wheel drive vehicle came to a 'screeching' halt.

"Everyone get out of the vehicle! Now!" both officers screamed with side arms drawn pointed directly at the three passengers.

Claude quickly raised his hands above his head in an international gesture of 'Don't shoot." Hilda began to imitate Claude's action, she reached into her purse and deftly slid a .38 caliber pistol into her waistband and slowly reached up and undid Claude's .38 fastener that gave him access to his own weapon.

"GET OUT OF THE VEHICLE!" came the harassing command again. Hilda and Claude held both their hands aloft in the 'Don't shoot!" stance.

Ivan awakened in horror, leaned up and peeked between the seats and eyed all the action in horror.

Claude attempted to speak in halting Russian responding to the Russian soldiers.

"SILENCE!! Where are you headed and what is your purpose for being here?" The Senior Officer demanded of Claude.

The colossal driver responded by haltingly stating they were headed to the Ukraine to deliver a 'message' to the Khrushchev family.

The Senior Officer glanced over at the Junior and shook his head in a negative manner. "Sir, we were given strict orders that no one passes through this concealed route without expressly written orders from our Russian High Command. You both will have to come with us to Moscow. You both are under Military arrest."

Rapidly and without hesitation, regardless that the two officers had their weapons directed at he and Hilda, Claude reached back and grabbed his revolver from his holster and instantaneously got off four rounds in instantaneous action.

Both Russian officers were hit by Claude's .38, but the Senior officer, as he was drawing his weapon had immediately and instinctively fired a shot directed at Claude. But in his reactive pain, the Russian officer grunted and screamed, then twisted, and the bullet intended for the Gargantuan one hit Hilda in the chest, killing her instantly.

Claude's marksmanship had been excellent. His fired shot had found their mark and hit both Russians in the head, killing them dead in their tracks. Claude immediately ran over and inspected both officers, reassuring himself that both were, indeed, dead. Then Claude jumped back to the prostrate body of Hilda, in stunned disbelief that the nursemaid was indeed dead.

Ivan situated in the back of the 4-wheel drive vehicle, blinked his eyes at Hilda, shocked at the surreal image before him.

Claude jumped back in the vehicle and pulled a distraught Ivan up into the front seat with him. He roared, "Ivan, this is absolutely horrible, but we must push forward to our destination outside of Kiev."

The large one looked over at the sobbing Ivan and solemnly declared, "Sorry son, but Hilda is… dead. I will take care of you now for the rest of our trip."

Ivan began to cry hysterically and crossed his arms over his chest and screamed, "NO!!!!!!!! take me home to Adolf Hitler and Eva Braun, my mother and my father !!!"

Claude slapped Ivan hard across the face with the back of his hand and then grabbed the youngster and pulled him within inches of his horrific face. "SHUT UP, IVAN!!" Claude then slapped the other cheek of Ivan and exclaimed again, "SHUT UP !!' Claude pushed Ivan against the seat and screamed, "Don't you ever argue with me ever again !!"

Ivan huddled tightly to the right side of the passenger's side area of the 4-wheel drive vehicle and sobbed uncontrollably. Ivan's dear sweet 'Nursemaid Hilda' who had comforted him for as long as he could remember was dead. And he no longer had his Mother Eva nor his father Adolf. Apparently, his new caretaker and chauffer, Claude was a mean, mean human Goliath.

Claude had made an enemy of Ivan when he had slapped the terrified, crying, grieving and distraught child. The remaining trip through the poorly charted terrain of Poland was rough and difficult as the 'disparate duo' pressed through and toward their objective of Kiev.

CHAPTER THIRTEEN

"ELVIS, do you need a break?" Pat Nixon quizzed her attentive guest, the King of Rock 'n Roll.

"No First Lady…...er, I mean …Pat." Elvis adjusted himself on the plush couch. "Thank you, thank you very much."

Both Pat Nixon and President Nixon giggled slightly with Elvis signature salutation.

"Elvis, again there is a reason I am being so diligent in portraying this portion of Ivan Hitler's youth. Be patient and you will see the reason I am being so meticulous telling this narrative.

Elvis merely nodded in understanding and agreement. The trademark sneer present in his lip was apparent as he made a motion with his hand for the First Lady to continue her story which the King of Rock 'n Roll was finding intriguing.

The First Lady nodded her head, acknowledging that Elvis was approving her continuance of the tale. Mrs. Nixon, taking a cue from the President's attempt at humor with his earlier shuffle across the room to refill Elvis' glass, actually attempted to mimic that famous lip sneer that Elvis was known for, as she launched into the Ivan Hitler story again.

"The backwoods trek for Ivan and Claude was tortuous regarding crossing terrain, but there were no further tragic human incidents. Ivan sat on his side of the riding seat with arms crossed tightly across his chest, his head turned intentionally away from the behemoth. Claude and the boy made progress toward their destination, the Khrushchev compound outside of the Ukrainian city.

Claude, who had mostly ignored young Ivan, finally turned to his indignant passenger and declared, "I am taking you to the residence of an especially important family in this country, AND they are secret friends with your Mom, Eva."

Ivan sat with crossed arms locked tightly over his chest and finally looked intently over at Claude. "Sir, I want to go home to my Mom and Dad, Eva and Adolf !!!" and with this pronounced declaration, Ivan stuck his right arm high in the sky in a 'Heil Hitler' salute.

"I have been given orders by your mom, Eva, and your father, Adolf, for your safety, to place you with Katarina Khrushchev. Ms. Katarina will take care of you!"

Upon hearing her name, Katarina quickly jumped up from her sitting space and interrupted Elvis' recitation of his Oval Office summit, and took a deep bow, swinging her right arm out to Dr. St. John and Elvis. As Katarina arose from her bow, her face turned a deep crimson shade as she realized she had acted impulsively at the mention of her name. "OOPS, sorry gentlemen. Elvis, please continue your dramatic story," Katarina murmured as she retook her seat.

Elvis nodded his head, "I return to my day in the Oval Office where First Lady Pat Nixon initially relayed this story about Ivan Hitler to me."

CHAPTER FOURTEEN

Pat Nixon sighed and stated, "Little Ivan was getting very, very upset."

"I want to go HOME! I want to be with my Mom and Dad, Eva and Adolf!" Ivan cried aloud, crossing his arms defiantly over his chest again. Large tears began to roll down his cheeks. "Hilda was my second mommy, and she is GONE!!" So, take me home…IMMEDIATELY!"

Claude slowly shook his head negatively again displaying that was nothing he could do "Sorry, young man, but I have been given strict orders to take you to be with Katarina."

The rest of the bone-jarring trip was spent in silence. Ivan sat in crossed-arm indignity, staring at the Eastern European country terrain as it passed. The silent duo's trail was marked in the same manner as when they left the outskirts of Berlin, bifurcated notched marks in trees lining the rough hewn trail. Ivan would, on occasion, glance at the behemoth driving the 4-wheel drive vehicle but the youngster's body language and total silence made it clear that he wanted distances to be kept.

It was a difficult trip with the 4-wheel drive slipping and sliding over the rough terrain. After two more challenging days of silent travel, the duo approached their destination outside of Kiev. Claude glanced at his map on occasion to make sure he was on the correct trajectory. "Look Ivan, that is the house up ahead." Claude pointed to a large sandstone rock villa situated on a hill above a meandering drive that led directly to the front door. "Young man, " he said with palpable resolve in his voice, "that is where Katarina Khrushchev lives and where are going to stay."

Ivan jumped to his feet and purveyed the sweeping brown colored Villa on the hill ahead of them and screamed at the top of his lungs…"I don't want Katarina Khrushchev…. I want to go home to Adolf Hitler and Eva Braun, my father and my mother!!" Ivan stomped his feet and jumped up and down ferociously. Claude ignored the raving youngster and cautiously turned toward the drive to the mansion, mentally processing how he would have to maneuver each turn with care.

"TAKE ME HOME! TAKE ME HOME! Ivan screamed stomping his feet on the seat.

Claude turned and grabbed his indignant young passenger as he pulled the rugged vehicle to the base of the winding driveway beneath the large Khrushchev estate. The gargantuan man then forcefully pulled Ivan directly to within one inch of his disfigured face. "Be QUIET Ivan, and calm down or I will slap and beat your bottom side until you beg me to stop!!!"

Tears cascaded down Ivan's face in such volume that it was dripping from his chin onto his chest.

Claude held Ivan close to his monstrous visage as he slowly motored and guided the vehicle up to the Villa. The behemoth glided the vehicle into a parking area, sighed with relief that the torturous trip was over, and turned to switch off the ignition.

"LOOK!" Ivan yelled, as down from the Villa walked two Russian uniformed officers. "Oh my God!" Claude sighed with exasperation as he observed the starchily uniformed men walking briskly toward the vehicle from 50 yards away.

The mammoth man turned to Ivan and grabbed the youngster by the shoulders and stared him right in the face. "Ivan, be quiet and sit here on the seat!"

"You going to take me home to my Mommy and Daddy ?"

Claude bellowed, "No, you little fool, you will be lucky not to be carted off to Moscow as a Germanic slave!" and then slapped Ivan across the face.

Ivan acted instinctively. Claude always kept his revolver on his hip as if in Military regalia. Ivan reasoned to himself…. "IT IS A TIME OF WAR AND IT IS NOW…OR… NEVER!"

Claude turned again back toward the oncoming officers. BANG! Ivan pulled the .38 revolver from Claude's holster and shot the ignominious Goliath directly in the right temple, killing Claude instantly.

Claude's huge form slumped forward over the steering wheel, blood streaming down from the wound, simultaneously splattering blood all over young Ivan Hitler.

The two officers glanced at each other as they heard the pistol discharge and began to sprint toward the truck, drawing their guns as they ran. Noticing the commotion, Katarina Khrushchev made a frantic beeline from the opened front door of the Villa, directly following the rapid footsteps of the officers.

The officers slowed their mad dash when they approached the vehicle and noticed the life-less body of the driver slumped over the steering wheel. Claude's lifeless eyes, frozen open, were targeted directly at young Ivan Hitler.

When the two officers approached the truck, they pointed their drawn weapons in a defensive action at the vehicle and the 6 year old, drenched in blood, sitting calmly by the dead driver, Claude.

The two officers glanced at the lifeless face of the slumped driver and both looked at each other in shocked recognition. "That's the infidel Claude, wanted everywhere in Russia!!" the two officers declared defiantly.

Ivan continued to sit motionlessly in the seat, ignoring the handgun on the auto floor that he had used to kill his tormenting abuser, Claude.

Katarina ran up behind the officers and stated, "Don't worry, it is just me, Katarina Khrushchev," as she patted them on the back. The threesome peered into the 4-wheel drive vehicle with cautious curiosity. They stared at the lifeless body of Claude.

"He killed himself when he saw you two officers approaching!!" Ivan suddenly declared as he pointed toward the huge body slumped over the steering wheel. Ivan nodded his head up and down fervently as if to further convince them that Claude had indeed done himself in when he saw that he was essentially surrounded by the Russian officers. He then pointed to the weapon on the floor, "He killed himself with his own weapon!"

Katarina seized the moment and began to talk persuasively to the Russian officers, nodding in agreement and supporting the blood-covered child's assertions. In a matter of minutes Katarina had talked her Russian officers into believing that the child's statements had to be true, that Claude had seen the two officers with guns drawn dashing towards him, and realizing how hated he was everywhere in Russia, felt he had no choice but to take his own life. The youngster, Katarina verified, was simply too young and innocent to have had anything to do with Claude's death.

Both officers looked at each other's shocked faces and it was obvious they were in consensual agreement about the event, and they felt Katarina was absolutely correct.

Katarina declared, 'The child is innocent of any of this," and she walked over to the riders side door, opened it, and placed her arms around the blood-soaked stoic Ivan Hitler.

The two soldiers looked at each other again and shrugged their shoulders in acceptance. "Our job is done, as the rascal Claude is dead," they declared with pride. Katarina turned and walked toward the officers and patted them both passively on their shoulders. "Yes, your job here is done," she acknowledged very matter-of-factly.

Then the beautiful Katarina walked calmly back to the 4-wheel drive vehicle and declared, "My family will take care of this poor indigent orphaned child," as she pulled the blood splattered Ivan from the vehicle. Then with a final look at the soldiers, "…and my family will dispose of this ……creature," pointing to the lifeless Claude with disdain. Then she turned, placed her hands behind each of Ivan's shoulders, and began to walk with the youngster up toward the Khrushchev villa.

The two soldiers glanced at each with a 'whatever' look, then turned purposefully and strode triumphantly towards their Jeep which was hidden back down the roadway. The Senior Officer declared as they both got into their vehicle, "Our job is done!!" With that final declaration, the Jeep fired up and the officers directed it back toward their Moscow destination. As vicious ol' Claude, who was despised by many, was dead, their job was indeed done.

Katarina glanced over her shoulder to make sure the two officers had indeed departed. Then the vision of beauty leaned over, her long brown hair flowing, looked directly into the eyes of the disconsolate, silent and stone-faced Ivan. "We have been expecting you, Ivan" Katarina exclaimed kindly. Then she put her elegant arms around the youngster and gave him a long, warm reassuring hug. "Ivan, you can tell me everything that has happened and we will talk about what will be going on later, but first, we have to get you up to the safety of the Khrushchev family estate villa. With that reassuring message, the model Katarina led the blood-stained youngster Ivan Hitler away from the horrific scene there at the vehicle, gently guiding him by his right arm up the meandering cobblestone drive to the imposing home and the safety it would provide for them.

CHAPTER FIFTEEN

"So, he shot and killed Claude his driver ?!?!?!" Elvis interrupted the First Lady, his face contorted in intrigue.

'Yep!" the First Lady responded glumly, nodding her head in acknowledgement. "AND… Elvis….please, please, remember there's a reason I'm telling you all of this in just intricate and exact detail !!"

President Nixon, interrupted, "Elvis, Pat is undeniably correct in that you absolutely must have a complete understanding of this person Ivan Hitler!"

Elvis looked first at President Nixon and shook his head in understanding, then turned back to Pat Nixon. "I did not mean to interrupt er.. Madam…er…" Elvis stumbled along…."I mean Madam…er… First lady…er, I mean… Pat !"

'Yes, 'Pat' is best, Elvis." First Lady Pat Nixon smiled broadly.

Elvis waved his hand in front of his body in a sincere gesture for the First Lady to forgive his interruption and to continue her story.

The First Lady bowed her head slightly in respect and continued. "Elvis, as you imagine given the tumultuous and tragic circumstances, Ivan Hitler and Katarina Khrushchev bonded as mentor and protégé. IMMEDIATELY!"

CHAPTER SIXTEEN

"And we DID bond… IMMEDIATELY!!" Katarina stood up in the Elvis' Monte Carlo villa and took a deep bow. Dr. St. John clapped his hands in appreciation. "The youngster needed help and support, that is very, very apparent."

Katarina smiled at Dr. St. John, then glanced at Elvis, "Sorry baby, I did not mean to interrupt your story. Please tell Dr. St. John everything."

Elvis softly said, "Alright," and pointed to his lovely Katarina as he continued the verbiage. "So where did I leave off?"

"About me raising Ivan!" Katarina declared and waved her hand in front of her motioning for Elvis to continue his story.

"Oh yes, that's right, I'll continue with how Katarina took over Ivan's parenting. And it is true, Katarina basically became Ivan's nanny, teacher and surrogate Mother….and basically…surrogate Father as well!"

There was World War II going on and folks had to adapt and survive. Ivan Hitler was always at Katarina's side. Ivan was taught Russian, and as Katarina was a bit of a genius at General Science, Ivan was given advanced classes in chemistry, electronics and the new expanding field of Nuclear Physics. The Khrushchev villa had a massive library covering all the fields of science that were also part of the curriculum at the University of Moscow. Katarina had been an outstanding student there prior to the onset of WWII.

Elvis smiled, "Katarina is not only a fashion model and is gorgeous, she also is an intellectual genius." Elvis beamed, obviously very proud of his girlfriend's intellectual capacity as well as her accomplishments. "Her physical beauty is.... well....very obvious." ANYWAY.... I'll return to my story as it was relayed to me by President Nixon and First Lady Pat Nixon.

Mrs. Nixon continued on about Ivan and his new mentor, Katarina Khrushchev: "The young Ivan Hitler was to be tutored by someone with an unusual desire to learn of all of the new scientific advancements of the day, and forward them on to her young student, Ivan. Katarina had risen to the top of her class at the University of Moscow. She was super intelligent, and had a special focused intelligence when it came to learning every aspect of the new expanding field of Nuclear Physics. As it would just so happen, Ivan Hitler also held super intelligence. He was a great student, and he too was instantly intrigued by the intricacies of the molecular aspects of nuclear science and physics. In fact, Ivan was a genius when it came to learning anything in regard to the Sciences. He may have struggled a bit with learning the Russian language, but it was as if his mind was a 'sponge' when it came to the sciences, especially all the molecular aspects and physics. Katarina thought it amazing how fast young Ivan picked up this complicated knowledge and built scientific skill sets."

She paused for a sip of Coca-Cola, then, continued, "The initial time span at Khrushchev villa estate actually seemed to fly by for the super intelligent Ivan, and since Katarina had taught him what was her primary interest as well, nuclear physics and anything related, she and Ivan bonded even more as their studies moved forward."

Mrs. Nixon stopped for a moment and gazed upward at the ceiling as if to gather her thoughts and ponder the gravity of her next statement, which was, "Then D-Day occurred and the end of the war in Europe was fast approaching. Then the horrible news for the family of the young genius Ivan came…"

Katarina walked into the library with a stunned countenance. Ivan declared, "Professor Katarina, you look so shocked and upset!!!" The youngster made this declaration as he prepared for that Monday morning classes.

Katarina approached Ivan in the Khrushchev library and sat down, trembling. Katarina, by her very nature, was almost always in a positive and upbeat mood. She was especially buoyant when teaching Ivan his Russian, science and nuclear physics. Katarina's dark brown eyes were streaked with tears. She continued to tremble as she sat there by Ivan's side. Initially Katarina avoided direct eye contact with Ivan. Eventually, she reached over and grabbed Ivan by his right hand.

"Katarina, what is wrong?" Ivan searched, staring directly up into her tear-stained face, trying desperately to extract some much desired information from his beloved tutor.

Katarina sobbed, then took a deep breath. "Ivan, I am afraid to tell you this…...but I think I am obligated to tell you something," she said reluctantly, slowly turning to her young protégé'.

Ivan scrunched his youthful face into a look of questioning concern. "WHAT, KATARINA?" He continued to try to extract some information from his tutor.

Katarina sobbed viciously then took a deep, long breath. "Ivan, I am afraid to tell you this…...but I believe I am obligated to tell you something," she said, finally turning to her student.

Ivan's face furrowed even deeper, until he finally asked again, "WHAT, Mommy Katarina??"

Katarina, in a halting, whimpering dialogue, sputtered, "Ivan, your Mother, Eva Braun, and your Father, Adolf Hitler…." Katarina simply could not look at her young student.

"WHAT…WHAT…WHAT about Mommy and Daddy?" Ivan screamed.

Katarina buried her head into her hands weeping, and released the horrible news to Ivan, "Your Mommy and Daddy are both ....dead." She grabbed Ivan's hand and squeezed it tightly. Ivan sat up erect and gazed at the downcast form of Katarina beside him crying her eyes out..

"IS THAT ALL....?" the petulant Ivan exclaimed with extreme nonchalance. With Ivan's non-feeling response to the horrible news that his Mom and Dad were dead, Katarina bolted erectly and turned directly to Ivan, looking at her prized student squarely in his dark brown eyes, shocked.

"IVAN HITLER, don't you care that your Mother and Father are dead?"

"Katarina, YOU are my Mother and my Father!!!" Ivan snorted, crossing his arms across his chest indignantly. "My mother, Eva Braun, and my father, Adolf Hitler, threw me away a few years ago when I was no more than a CHILD!" The 8-year-old scientific genius snorted in disdain, snapping his arms across his chest ever more tightly.

Katarina sighed, struggling to regain her composure. Bolting straight up and holding her head aloft, Katarina declared determinedly, "WELL, if that is the way you feel about things, Ivan, let's push forward with today's lesson on how the carbon molecules 4 valence electrons bonds work to join with so many other molecules!" Katarina tossed her long hair back and forth with exaggerated movement showing she was ready to proceed with the chemistry lesson.

"OK, Katarina," Ivan retorted sharply. "I am interested in the multiple bonds of the carbon molecule, BUT after pushing forward and reading in the textbooks from the Khrushchev library here, I have developed a gnawing inquisitiveness about the plutonium and uranium molecules and the radiation propensities of BOTH!!"

CHAPTER SEVENTEEN

"WHAT are you doing, Ivan?" Katarina asked as young Ivan had bent over the chair he was sitting on and was busy 'drawing' on his face. "I am going to be MORE world renowned than my father, Adolf Hitler!" Ivan declared as he jerked himself back into an upright position and stared Katarina directly in the face.

"WHAT have you done, Ivan?' Ivan leaned his head back to reveal the dark black moustache he had drawn on his upper lip emulating none other than Adolf Hitler.

Katarina quickly reached into her purse and produced a white handkerchief. "Come here, Ivan, I am going to wipe that OFF!"

Ivan snapped to his feet and declared…"NO, Katarina! Never !" I am always going to wear this drawn-on moustache to remind me, Ivan Hitler, that I am going to be MORE influential than my father. I AM GOING TO RULE THE WORLD !!"

Katarina stared in shock at the youngster. Staring at the mustachioed little one, she simply shook her head and sighed "Whatever, Ivan."

Ivan snapped his head forward and took his place back on his chair. "All right teacher, let's touch the carbon molecule as you suggest." But then Ivan held up the Nuclear physics book, "ON to the plutonium and uranium molecules...." Ivan then leaned back in his seat and pretended to stroke his 'faux' black moustache. "On to the powerful molecules that will enable me TO RULE THE WORLD!!!"

CHAPTER EIGHTEEN

"Gosh, that Ivan Hitler is a trip," Elvis sighed as he looked up with shock and disbelief at Pat Nixon. The First Lady shook her head in agreement. "Elvis, you are correct, and the story only gets worse!"

"Thanks for your patience, Elvis," President Nixon interjected, looking directly at the King of Rock 'n Roll. "The First Lady is taking adequate time to give you a very complete and comprehensive overview of Ivan Hitler and his full pediatric history."

Pat Nixon interjected, "It is vitally important for you to understand Ivan Hitler, considering what this man is going to politely ask of you," nodding her head toward President Nixon.

Pat cocked her head in an inquisitive manner as she looked over at Elvis. "OK if I continue this background story on young Ivan? You are still comfortable? Need or require anything, Elvis?"

"No Ma'am, I am good." Elvis sighed, "and I must admit I am intrigued by the story of Ivan Hitler…. he is beginning to sound like….for lack of a better word…. A PSYCHOPATH."

The First Lady smiled and shook her head in resignation…"Elvis, you have NO idea!" She sighed again, stating, "…and to reiterate, Elvis, this background and complete history MUST be understood…...so….with your permission, I'll move forward with telling you the complete Ivan Hitler story. Sounds silly in many ways right now Elvis, but again, you grasping all this is the reason President Nixon is having me tell you this story in such detailed minutiae, so bear with me just a bit longer and then I will turn the floor over to him and he will explain even further why you've been invited to the White House and the Oval Office."

Elvis shook his head again in agreement, "I understand Pat, please carry on with the story."

"OK, Elvis, then here I go again… So, Katarina Khrushchev morphed into a dichotomous blend of teacher AND mother figure as Ivan Hitler grew up. Katarina was brilliant in her own right, and her superstar pupil was blessed with such intellectual brilliance as well. Most grade school children Ivan's age might get interested in history or spelling. Not Ivan. Ivan Hitler loved science. and the more complicated the science was, such as nuclear physics, the more intrigued Ivan was. He absorbed science and particularly nuclear physics in a clear, concise and cogent manner that he was able to regurgitate that knowledge back to Katarina without hesitation. As Ivan considered himself Russian now, after the USA ended WWII with the atomic bombing of Hiroshima and Nagasaki, Ivan wanted to learn everything or anything available that could be studied about nuclear physics. AND with the ending of World War II things slowly began to return to more normal circumstances in Eastern Ukraine and Kiev. BUT…. Ivan Hitler was obsessed and driven. Ivan Hitler was incensed. Ivan Hitler was vindictive. AND…. Ivan Hitler was vengeful. Katarina stated that Ivan was often seen walking around with his hand held up in a Nazi salute stating demonically, "VENGENANCE IS MINE, SAYETH THE LORD!"

But Katarina also was emphatic that Ivan Hitler was brilliant… and Ivan Hitler was DRIVEN! Ivan Hitler was incensed. Ivan had lost his Mom and Dad whom he loved so much, and the young Fuehrer was forced to live in a country and culture that was not his own.

Ivan Hitler blamed only one entity for his situation...The United States of America. But even at his young age, Ivan was wise enough to direct his rage and hatred into a more productive pursuit than simply directing it at the USA. Ivan decided he would direct all this hostility into making himself a scientifically intellectual genius. By using this unbridled energy, he could acquire unlimited knowledge in the burgeoning field of nuclear technology and nuclear physics.

Katarina took delight in teaching the young 'genius' all she knew and all she could during their studies at the Khrushchev library in the Villa in Kiev. However, it soon became apparent to teacher and mentor that this isolated farm was not the place Ivan needed to master all the science behind nuclear physics.

After Katarina had imparted all of her knowledge to the young exponentially inquisitive student, she explained to him, "Ivan, to learn all that you want to know about Nuclear Science and Nuclear Physics, you either need to be in Oak

Ridge, TN, which of course, is IMPOSSIBLE……
Katarina wagged her head…absolutely positively
NOT…possible…OR you need to be in Moscow
to learn all YOU want to know!!"

"And Ivan," Katarina rationalized, "I can
certainly arrange for you to learn in Moscow. "NO
PROBLEM!" As Poland, Ukraine and other Eastern European countries were being absorbed by the
Soviet Union, it was just logical that Moscow was
the place for Ivan to be in order to learn.

Ivan continually pestered Katarina for the
next week until she too decided she had nothing to
lose by leaving Kiev and going to the University of
Moscow. Therefore both she and Ivan would go to
Moscow to learn and also to be with her cousin
Nikita Khrushchev.

So the dynamic duo of Katarina and Ivan
decided they would load up and head to Moscow
to learn all they could about nuclear physics and
the 'hydrogen bomb.' At 13 years old, Ivan was a
'budding genius,' and Katarina, at 21 years old,
was his mentor in 'all things intellectual' in a
manner of speaking.

The First Lady cleared her throat and took a gulp of her Coke. Sighing deeply, "to the next step in Ivan's growing process." Pat took another deep gulp of Coke and declared, "So now Elvis, let me tell you the story of the 'dynamic duo' and their tenure at Moscow University!

Elvis reciprocated and held up his amber fluid filled glass and nodded his head in invitation. "Please do!"

Pat Nixon walked behind the massive oak desk in the Oval office and pointed to Moscow on the giant world globe situated there. "Elvis, you have to remember now the 'Cold War' between the USA and Soviet Union was 'full speed ahead.'

She proceeded, "Katarina knew Ivan was different, but this 'aberration 'blossomed while in Moscow. In the Russian capital city, Ivan met Nikita Khrushchev, Katarina's cousin. Nikita, like Ivan, wanted revenge against the USA. Plus, Nikita wanted more, lots more. The future Soviet head of state wanted VICTORY over America."

Katarina and Ivan settled into a small apartment close to the University of Moscow located downtown in the Capital city of the Soviet Union. It was amazing, Ivan's quest of knowledge about the power of the atom had become addictive and obsessive. Surprisingly, the youthful Ivan and Nikita Khrushchev hit it off from the 'get go'. And amazingly Nikita wanted to know how the atomic and subatomic particles collided and exploded into the most powerful weapon the world had ever known. Katarina herself had grown more and more inquisitive about the power of these atomic and subatomic particles as well.

So, each of the trio had their individual desires. Katarina wanted truth and knowledge. Ivan truly, truly wanted revenge. Nikita wanted power. Nikita wanted to be leader of the world. Both Nikita and Ivan could attain their goals by harnessing this most powerful weapon ever imagined by man.

It was amazing how Ivan and Nikita built and exceptional rapport between themselves. This camaraderie was ignited when Katarina invited Nikita, her cousin, to dinner when she and Ivan were settling into their Moscow apartment.

"Ivan, this is Nikita!" A beaming Katarina introduced her balding, stout cousin to the mustachioed Ivan, whose dark hair and moustache were a compelling reflection of his father, Adolf. The duo approached each other in the small Moscow apartment as Katarina motioned the pair together.

"OH, MY GOODNESS !!!" Nikita declared as he shook Ivan's hand enthusiastically. "You are a spitting image of your Father, Adolf !!"

Ivan simply smiled and rubbed his black moustache dramatically and cordially replied, "Thank you, Sir."

"Nikita, Ivan. Please call me Nikita."

Ivan shook his head in agreement and declared, "Thank you for the compliment in regard to my father."

"Certainly, absolutely," Nikita stated.

Ivan continued to stroke his black-haired upper lip and proclaimed, "Nikita, I hear you are infatuated with the science of the collision of atomic and subatomic particles and the magnificent 'blossoming' of their collisions, just as I am."

Nikita Khrushchev smiled and reached up with his right hand and patted his balding pate. "Why, yes, I am, Ivan. Katarina told me that you were as intrigued and fascinated with atomic and subatomic structure and the possible worldwide consequences of understanding and harnessing the power of the atom as I am."

Then the two smiling comrades laughed a bit and Nikita affectionately grabbed Ivan by the back of the neck and pulled the youthful 'nuclear physicist' over to a small coffee table to the side of the apartment room. Nikita pushed Ivan down into the adjacent chair, then he pulled up a chair right next to Ivan.

Nikita looked at Katarina, and in Russian, said, "Пожалуйста, Катарина, можно нам водки?" ("Please Katarina, may we have a vodka?")

"OK, cousin," she replied, acquiescing to Nikita's request, as her cousin had climbed up the hierarchy of the Soviet power ladder and was a very important person.

By the time Katarina had turned and poured two shot glasses of Russian vodka and returned to the coffee table to serve Ivan and Nikita, the duo were already immersed in a detailed and comprehensive conversation concerning the various atomic and subatomic variations between plutonium and radium. At times there appeared to be a bit of a struggle to communicate, as Ivan still was somewhat of a novice at conversational Russian. The youngster was indeed a fast learner, but was still learning to master the nuances of the very complicated language.

But the pair had hit it off instantly, and she heard Ivan preaching enthusiastically about the unbelievable power created when hydrogen atoms were caused to collide... "INCREDIBLE! the mustached young man declared.

Nikita was seen bobbing his head up and down fervently in agreement. So intense had the discussion between the two conversationalists become that Katarina had to forcefully negotiate a position on the coffee table between them to set the vodka filled glasses down.

Katarina shrugged her shoulders as the two intensely conversing 'nuclear physicists' ignored her as she walked back to the small kitchen and began to prepare some dinner. Glancing briefly over her shoulder at Ivan and Nikita, she heard Nikita as he declared "Ivan, with that much power one could exact revenge... AND RULE THE WORLD !!"

Katarina yelled from the kitchenette, "Boys, it is almost time to cut the small talk and get ready to eat dinner!" The lovely brown-haired lady's admonition was ignored, not intentionally, but the discussion between Ivan and Nikita was morphing so rapidly into a joint diatribe about their knowl-edge of the incredible atomic world that they had no comprehension of anything else going on around them.

Katarina found herself actually getting a bit jealous of Ivan's and Nikita's new found intellec-tual relationship. Katarina had been Ivan's teacher and mentor. She had taught Ivan everything he knew. NOW….Nikita Khrushchev was unleashing a proselytization to Ivan that had totally captured the young man's cognitive attention.

Surprised at the jealousy this formidable intellectual interchange had invoked inside her, Katarina picked up the plates of Romanov noodles she had prepared and forcibly and intentionally plopped the noodle-laden plates down between Ivan and Nikita as a tacit demand that they stop their passionate discussion and pay attention to her presence.

To Katarina's chagrin, Ivan and Nikita barely looked up from this spirited diatribe. Both absentmindedly accepted their plates of food, but without even acknowledging the formidable effort that Katarina had gone to prepare this Russian delicacy. They simply pushed their plates aside and continued their boisterous banter of scientific intellectual verbiage about subatomic particles and the endless possibilities for power that this nuclear chemistry offered them. The discussion between each other was unremitting and incessant.

Katarina snorted in disgust, shrugged her shoulders in an 'I don't care' gesture and stomped her way back to a cubicle next to the kitchenette and began to consume her self-crafted gastronomic delicacy in isolated ambivalence. She watched in separated silence as Nikita and Ivan's conversation and pronouncements became more and more vociferous and enlivened. She actually stopped eating for a second, just long enough to whisper out loud enough, hoping Nikita and Ivan could hear, "You two are CRAZY!" as Nikita and Ivan's deliberations became ever more animated and gleeful. Needless to say, Nikita and Ivan, totally engrossed in their conversation, did not hear her.

"All this over a bunch of hydrogen and plutonium atoms!" the brown-haired beauty snorted, and resigned herself to eating her dinner in solitude and silence. Eventually she tired of the continued seminal lecture between the two 'atomic energy addicted duo' and migrated to her bedroom and left the two self-engaged men to their own devices.

CHAPTER NINETEEN

"Well gentlemen, that is going to have to do it for today." Pat Nixon declared as she glanced at her watch. "It is bedtime at the White House."

President Nixon shook his head up and down in accord. "ELVIS, this has been a long day. The First Lady is tired, and to be honest, so am I." The President stood up and reached towards the sky with his arms, yawning and stretching. "Walk with us, Elvis, and you can sleep here at the White House."

The rest of the night was uneventful, and as Elvis was exhausted also, he slept deeply. The next morning Elvis cleaned up and slipped out of his room and down to the Oval Office. Pat Nixon and President Richard Nixon were both sitting and awaiting the King of Rock 'n Roll's arrival. Both arose and smiled broadly when Elvis walked in. Elvis extended his hand and shook both Pat and the President's hands exuberantly.

"Elvis, before Pat starts the story back where we left off yesterday, I have this to say…" and to

Elvis' shock and surprise, the President swiveled his hips, playing an imaginary guitar, and in his best baritone and best Elvis impersonation began to wail, *"Minding my own business, drinking my daddy's juice, I swear I will never touch that stuff again...!"*

Elvis declared, "Mr. President, that is from Blue Hawaii !!"

Pat Nixon sprang to her feet and ran over and got in between Elvis and the President. "Let's all join in!" and the trio sang the rest of 'Beach Boy Blues" with glee.

"Blue Hawaii is my all-time favorite Elvis movie!!" the President proclaimed at the end of the triumphant rendition, clapping his hands together wildly and with glee.

Pat and Elvis smiled broadly and clapped their hands joyfully as well.

The First Lady then stepped to the middle of the Oval Office and declared, "OK, gentlemen, I hate to break up this love fest, but we need to get down to business!"

The President leaned over and hugged Elvis in a triumphant gesture of sincere appreciation and gratitude. Then President Nixon walked behind the wooden Oval Office desk and Elvis walked over to his customary place on the luxurious couch in front of the desk. First Lady Pat Nixon then walked to her customary place right in the middle of the Presidential seal rug. She bowed her blonde head and started to pace back and forth over the seal representing the highest office of the USA.

A scowl formed over the First lady's face. "OK, where were we? Oh, OK, that's right!" she exclaimed as she held her right index finger high in the air in a declaration she remembered where she had left off the story of Ivan Hitler and Nikita Khrushchev the night before. "Ivan and Nikita had become more than cursory friends, and when we left the story they were deep in conversation about the intricate mechanism of nuclear fission and the subsequent formation of nuclear weapons."

Elvis reiterated…." Correct, Pat, we are talking about Nikita Khrushchev the leader of the Soviet Union, aren't we?

"That's correct, Elvis," Pat responded. "The very reason or at least a part of the reason you are here is that Ivan Hitler became very close compatriots with Nikita Khrushchev, Premier leader of the USSR. So let me begin ...again," she said, smiling at her lyrical reiteration, adding, "..and keep in mind that this is a complicated timeline with many events that were shrouded in secrecy, so in some cases I have had to depend on reliable inside sources for certain details. Therefore, can we absolutely, positively guarantee every timeline or statement is totally accurate? Maybe not, but the President and I can assure you that the overall picture I am painting for you is. So, Elvis, pay very close attention to the next part of the story as it is crucial."

"I love the nuclear physics class at Moscow University Ivan, BUT," Nikita lowered his balding head dejectedly as he, Ivan and Katarina sat in the tiny student apartment sitting almost adjacent to the square where the university was located. Nikita shook his head, obviously very downcast.

"What's wrong, Nikita?" Katarina quizzed, clearly noticing that her cousin was extremely disappointed …. or something.

"The Government ministry is making me come into the Kremlin, insisting that I start to take Municipal classes, training me how to run the Russian government as well as the ENTIRE Soviet Union!" Nikita sighed and rolled his head again in disappointment. "I won't have time to attend class to learn more about the nuclear physics research and advancement in this exciting field."

"WHAT?!" Ivan screeched. "Brother Nikita, as we have discussed tonight, we are just now making such huge progress with the plutonium atom and the addition of the carbon molecule to both the hydrogen and plutonium atoms ...with the 4 bonds that can be attached, we can expand the power of the hydrogen explosion by possibly one hundred times beyond what it is now." He then jumped to his feet and shrieked excitedly, "They can't do this to me!" The young nuclear enthusiast stroked his jet black 'Adolph' moustache over and over with both hands, demonstrating his frustration and anger that his newfound compatriot Nikita was being yanked away from him.

As Ivan stood there in front of Nikita and Katarina compulsively fidgeting with his signature facial hair feature, it flashed in Katarina's mind that this had happened before to him when he lost his mother Eva and his father Adolf. Now he was losing his 'brother' Nikita in a similar fashion.

Katarina sensed Ivan's internal conflict and hurt and she jumped up and attempted to calm and placate Ivan, but unbeknownst to she and Nikita, a furor was building inside the black mustachioed iconoclast. Ivan began to jump up and down in rage and tears began to stream down his face. The 'jumping' in place had caused his dark black hair to streak down his forehead and he used his right hand to push the black strands back into place.

Then, oddly and unexpectedly, Ivan burst out into a musical tirade, and swiveled his hips as tears continued down his face... *"I've found a new place to dwell, it's down at the end of lonely street, called Heartbreak Hotel..."*

Nikita jerked his eyes away from the hip swiveling dark haired, mustached human tirade in front of him and glanced at Katarina quizzically. The Russian Premier then held up his hands in a manner that silently inquired 'what is going on?'

Katarina leaned over to her cousin and explained, "Nikita, Ivan has become a huge Elvis Presley fan, and he is showing his emotions by singing the hit 'Heart Break Hotel.' In fact, Nikita, Ivan has searched for a person to BE since his tumultuous childhood.... I believe HE THINKS of himself.... identifies himself...inside...as ...Elvis."

Nikita looked again at the gyrating Ivan in the middle of the apartment and simply shook his head in confusion. "Katarina, as you can tell, Ivan and I have grown close even though we have only known each other for a truly short period of time."

Nikita threw his hand out, pointing to the human dynamo attempting to mimic the Western World's Rock music icon, Elvis Presley. He tilted his head and looked again at Katarina and sighed, "...but cousin, duty and my country calls, and I have to go serve in the Kremlin in the Moscow. Just the way it is."

Then the cousins gazed back to the middle of the room as Ivan attempted to leave his pain of the loss of Mom and Dad and now a new friend, and gained even more enthusiasm for his sudden departure from the son of Adolf Hitler and his 'morphing' into the King of Rock 'n Roll, Elvis.

"Cousin Katarina, Ivan cares for you and respects you,. Please, please explain to him that Nikita Khrushchev MUST go and do what he must, as duty calls!"

"Ivan will get over it, Nikita" Katarina laughed softly as she nodded toward the gyrating dynamo performing mindlessly to his two-person audience still watching the solo performance.

"Yes, he will get over it Nikita, Ivan loves himself... AND he loves being...ELVIS......!!!"

Both Nikita and Katarina had to giggle as they looked on in amazement as the only known son of Adolf Hitler and Eva Braun continued to mimic the Western World's 'King of Rock 'n Roll,' Elvis Aaron Presley.

After a few more frenetic moments, Ivan began to titrate down from his musical, linguistic and physical mimicry of Elvis until he finally came to an exhausted halt. His newfound friend Nikita motioned for him to come and sit down and listen to him. Ivan shook his dark black hair covered head in agreement and came and plopped down, drained, next to his new best friend Nikita.

"Ivan, the news that I have to leave our beloved studies of nuclear fission is very, very disappointing for us, BUT…" Nikita held up his right hand in enthusiasm and announced, "I have a fantastic news bulletin to relay to you, Herr Ivan Hitler!"

Ivan tilted his head inquisitively. "What's that, Nikita?" he asked, showing deep respect for his newfound close ally, intellectual collaborator and study partner.

"The Kremlin is going to appoint you, Ivan Hitler, as head of the new nuclear fission task force project that is moving forward with great speed as we speak." Nikita held up his hands as if signaling a great victorious celebration. "The project is being spearheaded right this moment in a town called Chernobyl."

Ivan looked at Nikita graciously and stroked delicately at his thick black moustache. "Thank you, thank you very much." Unexpectedly and without saying anything else, Ivan turned and walked into his bedroom in the small Moscow apartment.

Nikita glanced at Katarina. She opened her eyes widely then tilted her head slightly. "Cousin, Ivan and I have grown close intellectually over the years, and all I can say about his behavior just now is that he is very, extremely moody."

Nikita looked at Katarina with eyes wide open. "Absolutely for sure, He is very moody isn't he, Katarina?"

Nikita, that is just the way he is." Then Katarina formed her hand into a fist and placed the fist under her chin in a pensive pose. "You know what you might do, Nikita?"

"What, Katarina?"

"Nikita, this may sound crazy…...BUT…." Katarina scowled her forehead and paused her thought process.

Nikita looked at Katarina intently. "Go on, Katarina…..What, what, what, what?!"

"Nikita, this will sound crazy. BUT… put Ivan in a night club in Kiev where he could play and perform the Elvis Presley music that he loves." Katarina then looked at Nikita and wiggled her forehead up and down in a 'what a brilliant idea, eh..?' fashion. "It may sound crazy, Nikita, but I swear, all Ivan does around this apartment is act like he is playing a guitar, swivels his hips and sings Blue Suede Shoes, Heartbreak Hotel, and Jail House Rock! Elvis Presley songs!!"

"I know Katarina, I have already heard from the professors and students that that's all he does in the nuclear physics lab at the University." To illustrate his point, Nikita held up his hands and shook his hips in full-blown Elvis mimicry. "The professors say that Ivan is brilliant with his nuclear research …. but ELVIS is all he talks about and mimics while he is at the University studying.

"So, how do you know all of this, cousin Nikita?" Katarina quizzed.

"I checked Ivan out before I came over here tonight. I always check out folks before I agree to have dinner with them. So did the KGB, cousin."

Katarina smiled, "Smart. Of course you had to."

"Everyone said he is brilliant; moody…but brilliant. And all they talked about was what Elvis song he performed the best,' Nikita declared and smiled wryly. He glanced briefly at the door hiding the moody Ivan, then looked back at Katarina. He offered, "What about *this*, cousin? We can set him up in a place in Kiev to sing and perform Elvis Presley songs at night, then during the day he can come and work at the nuclear laboratory program at Chernobyl!"

Katarina smiled broadly and bounced on her feet, clapping her hands together excitedly. "That is brilliant Nikita! Ivan will love it! An ELVIS venue in Kiev to perform at night after he has done his important nuclear research facility work that day. He absolutely loves to perform AND study and research. This is brilliant!!"

'Why can't you go with Ivan to Kiev, Katarina?"

"Nikita, as you know, Mom and Dad really, really need me here!"

Nikita intervened by putting both his hands on his cousin's shoulders. "Katarina, your country needs you. You have to help guide this scientific genius. As with many intellectually brilliant folks such as Ivan, they need a great deal of emotional support."

Both Nikita and Katarina glanced over at Ivan who was 'swinging' his hips Elvis' style, now oblivious to his friends.

"With the right support and direction, Ivan can help us to create the most significant atomic weapon on planet earth and can help the Soviet Union....AND me, Nikita Khrushchev, rule the World!!"

"Nikita, is Ivan truly that brilliant in regard to nuclear physics?" Katarina looked at her cousin with a perplexed and anticipatory countenance as Ivan continued to bounce up and down performing in front of an invisible audience.

"YES! Katarina, you recognize that I am a smart person, don't you?" Nikita quizzed his cousin.

"Of course, Nikita. Without question I know that you are brilliant. "

"Katarina, you know that Ivan's professor Martzo at Moscow is well schooled in nuclear physics, don't you?"

"I have heard Professor Martzo is brilliant."

"Katarina, Ivan truly has an unbelievable, incredible… indescribable… innate…. apparently God-given understanding of molecular physics and particularly how nuclear physics works." Nikita nodded towards the still entertaining mime and continued, "Last week Ivan explained to Professor Martzo his idea on how to make the nuclear fission process that we understand now by a simple yet ingenious plan that shows his incredibly innate brilliance. Katarina, Martzo says Ivan is a nuclear genius and our country has to put that genius to work …NOW!"

"OK, cousin…" Katarina nodded her head in understanding and cognizant agreement.

They both slowly and intentionally looked over their shoulders at Ivan who was continuing his performance in front of his invisible audience, rockin' and rollin' à la Elvis Presley, who was now audibly singing while rocking his hips back and forth and playing his imaginary guitar, *"....but I...can't...help...falling in love with you...!"*

In front of their very eyes, the son of Adolf Hitler and Eva Braun was deftly morphing into the Western Entertainment Icon, Elvis Aaron Presley.

"Yes," Katarina concluded, "I understand Ivan is a certifiable nuclear physics genius...BUT he also loves the music of the American Legend Elvis Presley.

Nikita nodded his head in agreement. "And Katarina, with that dark black hair inherited from his father, Adolf Hitler."

"And those deep seductive eyes from his mother, Eva Braun," Katarina added, looking at Nikita. Nikita stared back at his cousin. They both glanced at each other incredulously. Nikita and Katarina, both doing a double take, simultaneously exclaimed, "HE LOOKS LIKE ELVIS!!"

"Katarina, I will get the State to assign someone to help with your Mom and Dad. You MUST go to Kiev with Elvis…er…er, I mean… Ivan."

Katarina sighed and stated, "Nikita, you are correct, Ivan is a genius BUT I have to go with him to Kiev and watch over him."

Ivan continued his solo performance and got back to the lyrical verse that he adored so much, *"And I…can't…help…falling in love…with you…"* singing into his imaginary microphone as he rocked his hips in 'Elvis' fashion.

Katarina sighed "OK, Nikita help me to get someone to help my Mom and Dad and I will go with Elvis…" She rocked her head in dismay, "I mean IVAN…and I will take care of him in Kiev so he can work at the Chernobyl nuclear research facility…but Nikita, it will seem weird to have an Elvis Nightclub in Kiev."

"Not at all, Katarina. There are Elvis Presley impersonators all over the world now!" Nikita enjoined. "We will just have to get folks in Kiev and the Ukraine ready for a German-transplanted

Russian-imported version of the 'King of Rock 'n Roll!' With that convoluted protracted statement, Nikita and Katarina could not help but chuckle between themselves.

The cousins then turned their attention to Ivan being Elvis. Nikita clapped his hands together and declared, "Katarina, go tell Ivan the great news!" and nudged his cousin slightly forward toward Ivan. He then spoke in an elevated voice hoping to be overheard…... "I am positive he will be glad to go head up the nuclear research team at Chernobyl now that he knows you will accompany him AND he is going to have a nightclub that he can perform as Elvis Presley at night in Kiev!"

That statement caught Ivan's attention and he stopped being Elvis immediately. "WHAT?!" Ivan jumped around and stared at Katarina and Nikita with his eyes wide as saucers. "Katarina, did I hear Nikita correctly? We are moving to Kiev and I can be a nuclear scientist at the Chernobyl Lab during and the day…….and at night …."   he then began to dance around …...AND at night I will have my own night club to perform as the King of Rock 'n Roll…...ELVIS PRESLEY?!"

Katarina and Nikita looked at each and just smiled. Just as he had hoped, Nikita's statement had definitely caught the swivel-hipped Ivan's attention.

"Yes Ivan, you heard correctly," Katarina declared. "You, Ivan Hitler, can be a renowned nuclear physics scientist during the day......AND then at night.... you, Ivan Hitler, can be the 'King of Rock 'n Roll', ELVIS PRESLEY at his very own night club!!

Ivan shrugged his shoulders, tossed his jet black hair and screamed, "WHEN DO WE LEAVE?!"

CHAPTER TWENTY

That week, Ivan and Katarina loaded up all of their meager belongings into an old 4-door Mercedes and headed back west toward Kiev and Chernobyl. Katarina had an acquaintance who had picked them out an apartment on the Chernobyl side of Kiev. Ivan said extraordinarily little as he drove diligently toward their new home site and what lay ahead. Katarina would jump in her seat as she rode along and the black mustachioed one would spontaneously blast out in *Jail House Rock* or *Blue Suede Shoes*. Other than Ivan's occasional outburst in song, not very much was said between mentor and student on their long ride to destiny.

As they passed thru Kiev, Ivan slapped his forehead when they drove past an empty building on the front street of the main square. "Hey, Katarina,… right there…that will be a great place for a 'Red Elvis!' Ivan declared, nodding his head up and down to the silent rhythms he was still hearing in there.

Katarina quizzed, "Red Elvis?" and glanced over at Ivan with a curious look on her face.

"Yep…it just came to me…" Ivan continued to nod his head up and down with excitement. "Red for Soviet Union, and Elvis…for the obvious reason." Therefore, we will go with "Red Elvis."

"OK, great idea, Ivan!!" Katarina agreed. "Red Elvis' it shall be!!"

"Look up ahead, there is the apartment!" Katarina pointed out to Ivan.

The duo pulled the Mercedes into a space in front of the apartment building and began to unload their sparse belongings. It only took a few minutes to tote their clothing and incidentals up to the second floor apartment space that was located conveniently just outside of Kiev on the road to Chernobyl. Katarina and Ivan scurried around stashing their belongings, settling in quickly.

"OK, tomorrow I go to Chernobyl, but then afterwards, we go check out that space on the square for the 'Red Elvis' nightclub."

"You got it. Great idea, Ivan!" Katarina gushed. "We will have the Red Elvis night club up and running before you can say… KING OF

ROCK 'N ROLL!" Ivan smiled and nodded in agreement.

The next morning Ivan rolled out of bed and took care not to make much noise so as to not awaken a still slumbering Katarina in the adjacent room. Katarina had laid out a starched Soviet Union uniform for him, and Ivan pulled it arm by arm and leg by leg, as it was a snug fit.

Ivan drove the Mercedes up to the gated and guarded fence surrounding the large compound at Chernobyl. He was immediately saluted by the uniformed officer and was told, "Comrade Ivan Hitler, you may drive in directly and park in the space in front of the main office." With that, the guard saluted Ivan again, opened the metal gate and directed Ivan to the parking spot right in front of the office. Ivan got out of the Mercedes and walked to the front door of the large red brick building. He was surprised when an officer, Lieutenant Cherenkov met him. Officer Cherenkov was only slightly older than Ivan but saluted him immediately. Ivan saluted the officer in return.

"Comrade Hitler, please follow me down the foyer to the elevators that lead to the subterranean nuclear research facility." As the doors opened, the officer waved for Ivan to enter, then he followed and closed the doors to the elevator headed to the subterranean facility.

"Comrade Hitler, we are glad to have you here at our Nuclear Research Facility," Officer Cherenkov declared as he pointed the way to the elevators. "Comrade Nikita Khrushchev says you are the brightest mind on Planet Earth in regard to the nuclear fission process and the research of this new and unimaginably important technology. We are so honored to have you here, Sir," he stated crisply, saluting Ivan. Ivan smiled and boldly replied, "Chairman Khrushchev is correct. I am the savant of nuclear fission!"

As the doors to the elevator opened to the main lobby of the underground facility, Ivan took a step into the foyer. Then his mouth opened and in a stunned manner he simply mouthed, "WOW!" The size and scope of the underground facility was unbelievable.

Officer Cherenkov waved his arm in front of Ivan to imply 'let's explore the facility,' and boldly led the way. Ivan smiled and stared at the large centrifuges and other nuclear systems that lined the way to the check-in desk.

"Comrade Hitler, every day you report to the Nuclear Research facility here, please check in with Officer Adrianna Krakow."

Ivan's mouth dropped open as he saluted the stunning blonde officer, who looked him right in the eye and spoke succinctly, "Comrade Hitler, here is your identification badge that will allow you full admission to the underground facility." The statuesque blonde handed Ivan his credentials. Ivan took his badge and official documents from Adriana but he never took his eyes off her.

Officer Cherenkov smiled and respectfully tugged Ivan Hitler by the arm and directed him down the hallway. Ivan went, but his stare was centered on the check-in agent who looked more like a model than a military officer.

Cherenkov guided Ivan into an adjoining room that held an even more impressive array of nuclear testing equipment. Situated in the center of the room was an even more elaborate nuclear centrifuge surrounded by supporting and protective equipment.

Cherenkov gazed at Ivan and pointedly asked, "Comrade Hitler, do you understand the relevance and importance of all that is present in this room?"

Ivan looked at Officer Cherenkov as if he was askance of intellect. "OF COURSE!!" Ivan retorted; his mind finally diverted from the image of the beautiful Adrianna and directed to the job at hand. "Someone is at work and busy purifying our nuclear fuel!"

"Yes, that is correct, Comrade Hitler!" Cherenkov replied. "And the main reason, I believe, that Chairman Khrushchev has directed you to our facility is to use this equipment to help the Soviet Union identify, purify and collect the most powerful nuclear 'explosive material' the world has ever known!!"

CHAPTER TWENTY-ONE

Ivan spent the remainder of his first day at the Soviet underground nuclear facility studying ferociously and reviewing the equipment available to him. The dark-haired dark-mustachioed young man took three trips up the elevator to check out the main office AND to smile and shyly wave at Adrianna.

The day went by rapidly. At the end of the day the exuberant Ivan ran out to his vehicle and sang Elvis tunes constantly. He tossed his dark black hair repeatedly, especially when he drove by the empty building where he envisioned opening and performing there at RED ELVIS. Exhilaration mesmerized him all the way to the studio apartment. Ivan was SO excited by the day's events. He was going to be able to do his vitally important and world-altering scientific work and also perform and have fun at his new nightclub, RED ELVIS. Plus, he had perhaps met a potential female partner in the gorgeous blonde officer/underground nuclear facility manager, Adrianna.

Back in the apartment, Ivan's excitement did not dissipate. He was so enthused that he paced frantically back and forth and talked almost incoherently about the underground facility. Katarina tried to calm him down and tried to get him to eat something for dinner, both to no avail.

"Katarina," he said hyper-excitedly, "…this underground nuclear research facility just outside of Kiev in Chernobyl is incredible! The facility has all the equipment I need to do all this research that has been stored up in my cerebellum. I can now can test my hypothesis of the multiple valences of the ultra-heavy hydrogen-plutonium combination and put that postulate to work!"

"I know Ivan, I know." Katarina said with a smile. "That is why Cousin Nikita Khrushchev sent you over here!!"

Ivan laughed hysterically and sang *'Hunk-a-Hunk-a Burning Love'* ever louder as he gleefully trekked the apartment floor.

"BUT, I have even <u>more</u> good news for you, Ivan Hitler!!"

Ivan kept pacing the floor and broke out into an encore of *'Hunk-a hunk-a Burning Love.'*

"Good grief," Katarina muttered to herself. Not knowing what else to do, she simply reached over and grabbed Ivan by the belt in his pants and dragged him, singing, out of the apartment. The demure brown-haired beauty literally pulled him out as he bellowed his musical rendition. She dragged him all the way to the parked Mercedes, opened the rider's side door and flung him in. Ivan never missed a beat of music and continued his soirée.

Katarina walked over to the driver's door, opened it and plopped down by the 'singing Elvis genius', started the vehicle and drove down the road.

Katarina navigated the Mercedes to the front of the empty building on the square in Kiev. "Look, Ivan, Look !!' and she pointed to the newly painted visage that covered the window. 'Future home of …..RED ELVIS' Needless to say, <u>that</u> caught Ivan Hitler's attention!

"WOW!" Ivan screamed, twirling around in the Mercedes as they drove by the building. "Thank you, Katarina!" I really love the name RED ELVIS!" Ivan reacted happily. He was so overjoyed with RED ELVIS that he leaned over and kissed his mentor on the cheek. Ivan excitedly plastered his face against the Mercedes rider side window and stared, overcome with exhilaration at seeing RED ELVIS.

Katarina was happy that Ivan reacted in the positive manner that he did to RED ELVIS. Still, she was again surprised by a behavior from Ivan that was unexpected. She knew that Ivan would be excited, but the dark -haired dark-mustachioed one had acted like a 2-year-old kid.

"WOW, and kind of CRAZY!" Katarina thought to herself as she and Ivan returned to the apartment to retire for the evening.

The next morning Ivan was still riding a wave of excitement. He ate quickly and made a mad dash out of the apartment door. Ivan drove the Mercedes by the soon-to-be-opened RED ELVIS night club and pulled into his parking spot.

Later that morning as Ivan studied the nomenclature manuals and research and equipment guidelines at the nuclear research facility, he was approached by high-ranking uniformed officer.

"Ivan Hitler, I am General Hartno." Ivan jumped from his chair and gave the General a 'Heil Hitler' salute. General Hartno simply smiled and saluted Ivan, then extended his hand, eliciting a firm handshake from Ivan. General Hartno waved his arm in front of Ivan as a signal for him to walk forward. "First, Ivan, I want to formally welcome you to the most sophisticated nuclear research facility on Planet Earth."

As the two men walked forward, Ivan declared, "This place is huge and unbelievably exciting!"

The General signified his agreement with a nod and the two men walked forward through the underground facility. "Ivan," the General declared, waving his hand in front of them, "...this place is larger than a soccer field." As the two paused, the General continued, "...and Ivan, I reiterate, There is no more sophisticated nuclear research facility on Planet Earth." General Hartno stopped in front of the large nuclear centrifuge situated almost in the middle of the room. Speaking in a sober tone, he said, "Ivan, you were referred here to us by your chemistry and nuclear professors at the University of Moscow." The General then spread his feet apart, standing firm and upright as if to let his body language emphasize his seriousness. "We are undertaking the most complex and complicated nuclear research concerning the most powerful weapon on Earth. Ivan, we will need your help and cooperation. The hydrogen bomb is the most powerful weapon known to man now. We here at the underground nuclear research facility intend to make a weapon at least ten times stronger, and with everyone's help, make one a hundred times stronger than what is now available."

Ivan showed no expression of reaction, but stood firmly in place and pensively stroked his dark black moustache as he almost imperceptibly nodded his head in agreement.

General Hartno paused briefly to read Ivan's face, then continued, "Our nuclear centrifuge and accelerator is the most advanced in the world, bar none!" The General then pointed at the whirling centrifuge and the buzzing accelerator, stating,

"Ivan, with this equipment we can have the most powerful weapon on Planet Earth !!'

Ivan snapped his thin body erect as he pushed back a thick lock of ebony hair that had fallen over his forehead, and declared decisively, "I think I have the solution to the problem, General Hartno!"

General Hartno's thick black moustache seemed to stare at Ivan …and for a brief second Ivan flashed back, and his emotional memory carried him to his father Adolf Hitler's arms. Then he shook his head to clear the imagery and returned to the present just in time to hear General Hartno quiz him, "Ivan? Ivan Hitler, are you here? Are you with me?"

Ivan caught himself struggling a bit as he fought back tears….then the young nuclear genius pronounced proudly again, "General Hartno, yes, I do think I have the solution to the problem that is presented to us!" He collected himself totally and turned directly to General Hartno. "It is my belief based on my research that if we can increase the amount of nuclear bonds in the explosive plutonium material, then we can dramatically and exponentially increase the power of the nuclear explosion!"

Hartno stood tautly upright as now it was his time to be somewhat taken aback at the audacious statement from Ivan. "So…young Ivan Hitler, how do we increase the bonds of a particle as small as an atom?"

Realizing he had captured General Hartno's attention, Ivan flipped his black hair haughtily, stepped back from the General slightly, declaring as he turned and pointed toward the humming nuclear centrifuge, "I believe this machine, the nuclear centrifuge, is fundamentally the key." Ivan continued to jab his pointed right index finger at a large cylindrical turning mechanical apparatus.

The General still was at extreme attention, and Ivan could tell by how Hartno's facial features and eyes were expanded that he was impressed and captivated by Ivan's deep knowledge and overall thought process.

Hartno cleared his throat. "So, Ivan, you are telling me that if we can get a bond……." Then the General relaxed his posture slightly and demurred…. "So… young Hitler… explain to me E X A C T L Y what you are saying." With that, General Hartno crossed his arms across his chest.

Ivan nodded, realizing it would be best to put his exceptional linguistic skills to good use and explain his supposition and hypothesis in the simplest manner possible. "General Hartno….as you are well aware; all a 'bond' is between atoms is stored energy… or, in other words…stored POWER."

The usually stoic General toggled his head in acknowledgment that he agreed with the young man's statement, and Ivan continued, "If we can make……or ascertain with absolute certainty that the plutonium atoms we are splitting have more interconnecting bonds, then… when our weapon explodes……"

Ivan then turned his face directly toward General Hartno as if allowing him a moment to understand and absorb his hypothesis… "Or… the interconnecting bonds between those atoms rupture…THEN …. MORE energy will be created and a larger explosion is the end result! That is the Ivan Hitler hypothesis on how to create a much more potent and powerful nuclear weapon…… increase the nuclear bonds between the atoms." Ivan stroked his dark moustache in self-satisfaction as he finished his explanation.

General Hartno sighed, "Ahhh…I see," and shook his head up and down to show agreement.

Ivan, sensing that the General was coming around to his theories, continued, "The key is to use that state of science and our centrifuge to produce the hydrogen or plutonium atoms with more nuclear bonds so they have more power!"

Ivan stood back and declared decisively, "General Hartno, the MORE the nuclear bonds … the MORE nuclear power !"

Ivan and the General turned and looked at the nuclear generator and centrifuge. General Hartno then leaned back and sighed, "Ivan Hitler, this hypothesis and resulting explanation of the potentiality of the idea that you have thought of are precisely why my friends in Moscow have sent you to me !"

CHAPTER TWENTY-TWO

Ivan Hitler and General Hartno continued their discussion for another hour. When they parted ways that evening they felt like they had made potentially huge strides for progress at the nuclear research facility.

Ivan had explained some other theories that he felt were relevant and the General seemed truly excited with the potential. The General and Ivan shook hands and bid each other 'adieu.'

General Hartno stated as they were both parting, "Ivan let us start putting your theories to the test as soon as possible."

"Yes, sir , General Hartno!"

Smiling deeply and feeling aroused inside, Ivan piled into the Mercedes, fired it up and headed toward Kiev. Ivan motored rapidly toward his next project, RED ELVIS. As Ivan pulled into the parking spot in front of the future RED ELVIS, he was pleasantly surprised at the progress that Katarina was making.

Ivan strode inside and was gratified to see Katarina directing a couple of workers to build a stage upon which 'Elvis' would perform. She was also busy putting together of a portrait of Elvis on the back wall behind the bar area.

"Wow Katarina, this is going to be great!"

"Thank you, Ivan!" Katarina declared as she continued to paint a midnight black lock of hair on the 'Elvis' portrait.

"And by the way, Katarina, there is a piece of equipment at the underground facility that is fascinating. I can't wait to tell you everything!"

Katarina glanced quickly over her shoulder and declared, "That is great, Ivan." But the tawny-haired beauty continued to paint on the 'Elvis Fresco' and kept her workers busy completing the work on the stage.

Ivan looked at the painted portrait of Elvis Presley on the wall and instinctively stroked his dark black moustache. "Katarina, should I shave my moustache?" he asked, pointing to the portrait of Elvis that she was completing.

"Yes, maybe, Ivan."   Katarina shook her head positively.   "You would definitely look more like Elvis if you shaved it!"

Ivan continued to stroke his moustache. "But I like my facial hair, Katarina."

Katarina pointed again to the moustache-less figurine of Elvis she was painting. Then she pointed to the large red sign emblazoned on the front window. "Look who you are portraying in RED ELVIS, Ivan. ELVIS AARON PRESLEY!" Katarina stated emphatically. "ELVIS never wore a moustache "

"But why, Katarina?" Ivan whined.

"BECAUSE. in here you will not be General Hartno …...nor will you be Adolf Hitler. In RED ELVIS, you will be Elvis! Shave that moustache so you can be and perform as Elvis !!"

Ivan looked at the enlarged Elvis portrait that Katarina was continuing to complete and then glanced again at the front window. "RED ELVIS," he muttered under his breath as he again stroked his beloved moustache. Ivan's moustache was his homage to his father. His moustache was a constant reminder of how much he loved his dad. He sighed deeply and muttered to himself, "..this is going to be a hard decision for me to make."

Ivan sighed again and then slowly began to swing his hips and softly started to sing 'Jailhouse Rock.'   Then he smiled and began to strum an imaginary guitar.   Katarina paused her painting and looked back over her shoulder and smiled. "That is correct, Ivan, BE ELVIS, keep on singing. Keep practicing. We open RED ELVIS in 1 week and we need you to be ready to Rock 'n Roll!"

As if to encourage on a deeper level, a visual level, the stunning Katarina seductively rolled her hips in rhythm. Ivan sang 'Hound Dog' loudly as he slid his feet over the floor and strummed ever harder on his imaginary guitar.

The rest of that week, Ivan would stop by the RED ELVIS as Katarina and the work crew continued their work toward opening. Ivan loved the stage and the elevation it was going to give him over his audience. The 'pretend Elvis' would sway and swing and swashbuckle his way through the 'imaginary' audience as he practiced every Elvis song he knew.

After the work and Ivan's practice was over, Katarina and Ivan would head to the apartment and immediately fall to sleep, both weary from the day's grind. Ivan was up early and off to the underground nuclear research facility, and then, per routine, stop by the under construction RED ELVIS and parlay his time into the Elvis review he was going to present to the audience.

Katarina did catch Ivan up after seemingly retiring for the evening. She would hear him humming to himself some Elvis song rendition. Katarina would then watch and observe him in total anonymity. He had no clue she was observing him.

Strangely, he would hum a few Elvis tunes, then would turn to a workbook he had started to keep by his side constantly. It appeared he was working on lengthy and complicated nuclear-based algebraic algorithms. Ivan was so fervent in some of his mathematical computations and derivatives that he did not notice Katarina staring at him from her cracked open bedroom door. Katarina knew

Ivan well enough that she knew he was deeply involved in some sort of tangential mathematical nuclear equation that he was obsessed with at work. Ivan was using his slide rule to determine huge numerical calculations which he would then diligently and painstakingly transcribe the results of into his private workbook.

Each day was the same for Ivan. Get up early and go to work at the underground nuclear research facility. Then afterwards he'd drive the Mercedes and stop at the soon to be opened RED ELVIS to practice his Elvis portrayal show, then he and Katarina would go home, and ostensibly Ivan would go to sleep, only to get up about 2am and work diligently on his nuclear algebraic calculations in surmised privacy. Except that Katarina observed all of this from the stealthy sanctity of her bedroom. Katarina knew Ivan well enough to know that he was truly onto something of extreme importance in regards to his nuclear research. He was obsessed. But Katarina observed that Ivan was MORE than obsessed with his nuclear research. He was mesmerized. Even though Ivan could be strange at times, Katarina knew that with Ivan's underlying super intelligence, he was developing something that he felt was of huge significance in regard to nuclear physics and atomic science.

Friday before the Saturday night premier opening of RED ELVIS went as usual. Ivan headed out to the research facility. Katarina headed out to RED ELVIS to put finishing touches on the interior. Ivan stopped in the night club after work to polish up every aspect of his Elvis Revue show. Afterwards, like always, Katrina and Ivan headed to the apartment. Katarina thought Ivan was very quiet considering he was about to premier his pride and joy entertainment revue the next night.

Ivan walked straight up to Katarina and in a profoundly serious and almost stern manner, stated, "Katarina, sit down, please" as he pointed toward the small kitchen table.

Katarina sat down somewhat reluctantly and furrowed her forehead in a questioning manner as she replied, "What is it, Ivan?"

"Katarina, I have some things I want to tell you and to explain to you."

"OK, Ivan, I am listening," the slender framed looker said as she pulled her chair around so she could see Ivan better.

Ivan stood his ground and cleared his throat. "Katarina, in the very near future, I will have to accompany General Hartno on the Eastbound freight train to Siberia to work on our new project."

Katarina nodded her head. "No problem, Ivan, I can close RED ELVIS for a few nights and come with you guys…"

"NO…NO…NO," Ivan exclaimed, shaking his jet black 'Elvis hairdo' (accompanied now by long sideburns) in a negative manner. "You don't understand Katarina, this is TOP SECRET….!" He continued to shake his head negatively. "You CAN'T go!"

Katarina crossed her elegant arms across her chest and sighed in protest. "Ivan, I have taken care of you since you were a kid!"

Ivan continued to shake his head negatively. "Katarina, this is nothing personal. This truly is a TOP SECRET scientific Soviet project!"

Ivan persisted with his head shaking...."NO ONE is allowed to go accompany staff on these scientific expeditions except the folks utilized at the underground research facility." Still forcefully shaking his head 'no,' Ivan reiterated, "NO ONE!"

Then Ivan looked squarely at Katarina with his right eyebrow twisted in a 'don't doubt my word' countenance.

Then to release the tension between the longtime compatriots, Ivan relaxed his personal presence just a bit and placed a sneer in his lip à la 'The King of Rock 'n Roll.' Ivan then began to speak in a more relaxed and explaining manner, "Look, Katarina. "These trips and expeditions could be very dangerous, as we have to do some..." Ivan again cleared his throat a bit... "...*experiments*. We have to go to the isolated areas of Siberia as these locations are the only safe place to conduct these....experiments."

"Ivan, You mean you are going to test nuclear weapons and explosive devices?" Katarina crossed her arms across her chest even more tightly in protest.

Ivan's facial expression relaxed even more. "Katarina how do you know we …er…. MIGHT …be exploding nuclear weapons?" Ivan tilted his head to one side revealing perplexity in Katarina's knowledge.

"Hey, I am NOT an idiot, Ivan." Katarina exclaimed as she kept her arms tightly locked across her chest. Leaning forward, she exclaimed vociferously, "WHAT did we work on together constantly for almost four years at the University of Moscow…?!"

Ivan relaxed even more AND actually allowed a smile to spread over his face. "SHHHHH.....Katarina," he whispered, putting a right index finger across his lips while looking around the small apartment as if someone might have slipped into their tiny apartment and was listening to and spying on them. "Shhh…." Ivan reiterated with his finger placed sternly across his mouth signaling Katarina needed to be silent about anything he had just told her. Then he stepped forward and placed his right index finger across Katarina's lips. Ivan's countenance twisted into a serious look, and he continued, "Katarina, you do not want to bring us any problems with your bountiful nuclear knowledge…AND…with what I just told you."

"OK, OK, Ivan,…I certainly understand! Remember, I am a Khrushchev!"

Ivan waived his hand in appreciation and acquiescence. "OK, Katarina." So, can we please have fun at the Grand Opening of the RED ELVIS tomorrow night?!" Katarina's beautiful face smiled and mouthed, "Of course."

"Let's go have fun," Ivan continued, and then his countenance turned serious again, "BUT …we absolutely MUST keep our mouths shut about any of the work I am doing at the Chernobyl underground nuclear research facility." Ivan did his best to be upbeat, but continued solemnly, "the KGB is at the research facility every single day that I go in to work. The KGB will be on the train on our excursion to Siberia when General Hartno directs us to go do our experimental work. General

Hartno has warned me repeatedly to be silent about our very important and very SECRET work I am proceeding with at the facility.

Katarina rolled her eyes in exasperation. "OK, OK, OK," the fair-haired Venus exclaimed. "I GET IT! I will not say a single word about any of this!"

Katarina took her slender right index finger and propped it up demonstratively against her luscious lips to demonstrate she would be silent. She then sighed softly, tilted her head and replied quizzingly, "But Ivan, can we still enjoy and have a great time with you playing your Elvis Presley music at RED ELVIS every weekend that you are here?"

Ivan smiled and moved his head and hands in wild enthusiasm. "Yes, Katarina we can and we will!" Ivan's eyes opened wider with excitement. "Amazingly, after General Hartno discussed me performing my Elvis Presley impersonator revue rendition at RED ELVIS with the KGB, they all love the idea!

"Their exact words were that being an Elvis Presley impersonator will actually deflect attention from my REAL and IMPORTANT scientific work at the underground research facility. The KGB says it makes me look like a 'Western idiot from the USA' instead of the nuclear genius that I am." Ivan poked himself in the chest with his extended index finger showing that the KGB meant they had him pegged for being a ...GENIUS.?

With all the talk and explanation…. the 'ice' between Ivan and Katarina about Ivan's secret and clandestine nuclear research trips to Siberia was broken…...and forgotten. They both laughed and soon found themselves reminiscing how Katarina had to hold Ivan as a child to reassure him and help relieve his stress, and that all of the horrors he was experiencing would be gone.

CHAPTER TWENTY-THREE

Early the next morning at the underground nuclear research facility, General Hartno approached Adrianna. "Adrianna, let me talk to you before Ivan Hitler gets here." The statuesque blonde nodded her head in understanding. "Yes sir, General Hartno."

General Hartno led the way for them to enter his office and closed the door behind them silently. Speaking in a hushed tone, he said, "Young lady, it is our duty as underground KGB agents to keep our eyes on Ivan Hitler AND… his mentor that he resides with… Katarina Khrushchev."

Adrianna, standing in front of the General, tilted her head in a puzzled manner, allowing her long flowing blonde hair to dangle over her right shoulder. "I truly understand keeping an eye on Ivan….as you know…that job is the main reason I have been located here at the underground nuclear research facility…." then opening her bright blue eyes widely, Adrianna continued, "…but the lady he occupies the apartment with…Katarina…she is a Khrushchev. She is cousin to the prominent Nikita Khrushchev.”

General Hartno glanced bruskly at the long haired blonde. “Adrianna, listen to me…” the General demanded sternly, “Katarina Khrushchev is part of the family tree that had connections, and part were strongly affiliated with the Western allies and the USA in World War ll.” The General sighed….”Whether we like it or not… Katarina Khrushchev must be placed under observation and close scrutiny….AND, I have directives from Moscow concerning you and Ivan Hitler…” the General began to waffle and hesitate.

“General Hartno,” Adrianna interjected, “I have been sent by my superiors in Moscow to initiate relations…. undercover relations, so to speak, with Ivan Hitler, so I can keep very, very close tabs on the son of Adolf Hitler and Eva Braun.”

“Er…well…” the General muttered, ”How is that task proceeding?”

Adrianna smiled broadly. The model took off her baseball style Soviet cap with the red star emblazoned on the front, allowing her long blond tresses to cascade softly around her shoulders. Adrianna deliberately made the effort to wave her long golden locks triumphantly. "I believe I have young Ivan under my spell," she cooed as she blinked her gorgeous sky blue eyes rapidly. "I have Ivan Hitler wrapped around my little finger, General Hartno."

Adrianna pointed to a side room adjacent to the large soccer-sized main research facility. The blonde blushed as she continued, "General, I have taken cues from the CIA and the Germans and worked 'under cover' to get Ivan Hitler under my spell, so to speak. AND...General, I have lots of information going to the KGB as we speak."

"Great !!" General Hartno exclaimed as he shook his head up and down in a positive nature.

"Don't worry, General. Like I said, I have Ivan wrapped around my little finger," and the blonde wiggled her end right pinky to demonstrate her statement.

"AND I agree, Adrianna to let Ivan pose as this Elvis Presley impersonator at RED ELVIS, but you must keep Ivan under your spell at all times."

Adrianna gazed intently at Hartno with her piercing blue eyes, and whispered, "Oh, I will General. I most certainly will."

General Hartno shook his head and stated emphatically, "Believe it or not…. IVAN Hitler is a scientific genius. His work at the underground research facility is vital to the preeminence of the Soviet Union in the World!"

Adrianna shook her long golden locks again elegantly and seductively said, "Don't you worry, General… I have Ivan Hitler right where we want him."

"OK, young lady, please accompany the young genius Ivan on every trip to Siberia …. or wherever else he may want to go. Please keep him under observation at the night club.

"RED ELVIS" Adrianna interjected.

"Oh…I did not know the name of the joint. Good deal, but try not to alert Katarina Khrushchev to yours and Ivan's relationship."

"Of course, General, I understand. I will keep Ivan controlled." And with that statement Adrianna slowly and carefully gathered her long locks back under her baseball style Soviet baseball cap with the emblazoned red star on the front.

"You will report anything of importance or substance DIRECTLY to me, Adrianna!"

With that, the statuesque blonde KGB agent saluted General Hartno. He smiled slyly and also saluted Adrianna smartly and briskly.

CHAPTER TWENTY-FOUR

"Good morning, Ivan!" General Hartno exclaimed as the elevator doors to the underground nuclear research facility opened, and out walked Ivan Hitler into the extensive research facility operation. Adrianna silently and quietly retreated into her private office space so the two men could converse privately.

General Hartno stood smartly at attention and saluted Adrianna as she disappeared into her private space. Then General Hartno turned to give all of his attention to Ivan. He saluted Ivan sharply and questioned, "Comrade Hitler, how is your undercover role as the Elvis Presley impersonator at the nightclub…. I believe it is to be titled RED ELVIS…going?"

Ivan was somewhat surprised at this line of conversation but smiled broadly at the General's interest in his role as the sole Elvis impersonator in Kiev. "Things are going great, General Hartno!" as Ivan promptly returned the rigorous salute to his commander. "As a matter of fact, General, we open RED ELVIS tonight and I will give a rendition of my Elvis Presley impersonation!"

Adrianna slipped out of her office and stood a few feet away from General Hartno and Ivan as they talked excitedly about the upcoming tribute performance.

"Yay!" Adrianna clapped her hands together and stepped forward to the two men. "I can't wait to see that side …the Elvis side…of Ivan Hitler!"

Ivan looked backward in a somewhat askance and shocked manner at the blonde with the Soviet ball cap on. "What…...you're coming to see me tonight at RED ELVIS?"

Adrianna jumped up and down while smiling broadly and clapping her hands together excitedly…"Yes, of course, I am coming tonight! Can't wait.!"

General Hartno took a step toward Ivan and intervened, "Yes, Elvis….er…..er…I mean Ivan!" Pointing at the blonde officer with the Red star adorned Soviet baseball hat… "Adrianna has to be there…. someone HAS to watch your back. Ivan your work here at our nuclear research facility is that important!" Then General Hartno turned and strode to his office.

Ivan blushed! Slightly dark-skinned, à la his dad Adolf, still the redness showed through his facial complexion. Ivan had never performed for the gorgeous Adriana before and it embarrassed him somewhat to think about the 'Movie Star' blonde being in the audience.

Adrianna seemed to read Ivan's mind and understood his trepidation. She patted Ivan on the shoulder and exclaimed, "Ivan, don't worry," and reached forward and hugged him and whispered in his ear, "Our personal relationship can never be revealed. Please do not worry!"

The blonde stepped back and held out her right hand "We are two proud soldiers… in service of the Soviet Union!" Adrianna grabbed Ivan's free hand and saluted him with her right hand.

General Hartno had walked back from his office, and overseeing the action between Adrianna and Ivan interjected, "That's right, Ivan," pointing at the blonde model. "Adrianna is to guard over you whenever and wherever you are in the public." General Hartno continued in a solemn and declarative manner, "Ivan, your work is that vital to our country. Your true relationship will never be revealed outside of the nuclear research facility family." And with that, the General strode back to his office.

Ivan looked at Adrianna and placed his open right hand over his mouth. With wide open eyes he whispered to his blonde lover, "HE KNOWS?!" His face contorted with worry and concern.

Adrianna grasped Ivan by the shoulder and pulled him to her and clasped her long arms around him. "IVAN, do not worry. General Hartno wants us to be very, very close. That way we will be safe. "Adrianna kissed Ivan's forehead.

"Sweetheart, we just have to be secretive and confidential about our relationship when we are in public….that's all.

Ivan's eyes were as big as saucers. The black haired one simply shook his head in under-standing and agreement.

Adrianna smiled. and declared...." You are Elvis...you should know this saying better that anyone....it's just like in the town you love..."WHAT happens in Vegas...STAYS IN VEGAS! Same thing with us...it is all confidential baby. Let me hear you say it, Ivan...!"   Ivan shook his head and scrunched his face. "You mean what happens at the research center....stays at the research center?"

"EXACTLY!" Adrianna exclaimed as she grabbed Ivan and kissed him squarely on the lips.

"EXACTLY!" General Hartno exclaimed as he peeked out of his office door and saluted both Ivan and Adrianna curtly then disappeared again behind the door.

Adrianna looked at Ivan and tilted her head and stated, "I got this covered Ivan, leave everything to me.!" Then the statuesque blonde grabbed young Ivan and kissed him firmly on the mouth again. Then she began to pull on his arm and directed him toward her office. "Don't you want to retire to our room for 30 minutes and be alone before we begin our work......and remember, we go to RED ELVIS tonight to see your premiere!

Ivan seemed to shyly 'giggle' a bit as he looked around to make sure no one was present to see them. "Of course," Ivan declared when he saw no one was around …that they were alone. Adrianna always made Ivan Hitler deliriously happy when they were alone together, and the blonde played her 'undercover' role. In fact, and Ivan had decided he was never going to tell Adrianna this, but the Hitler youth had become deeply enamored and smitten with the beautiful blonde. Ivan had actually conceded to himself he had probably fallen in love with Adrianna.

"Come on," Adrianna whispered. Then the buxom blonde tugged Ivan into the side room and 'physically and passionately satisfied' the 'young genius' before their long day at work at the nuclear research facility.

Later that day Adrianna ran up to Ivan who was sitting immersed in his nuclear research work at his cubicle close to the large nuclear centrifuge. "Ivan, you have got to get ready and head to RED ELVIS for tonight's debut show!"

Ivan looked up from his manual and research log and his dark eyes lit up in excitement. "Wow, the time passed so fast !!" he declared as he brushed his dark black cropped hair just like the 'King of Rock 'n Roll.' "Thank you Adrianna, Thank you very much," Ivan stated, jumping up from his chair. As he was scurrying out the door he glanced back over his shoulder to ask his beautiful blonde companion, "Adrianna, are you are going with me to RED ELVIS?"

"Yep…. I will ride along!" she cooed.

"Of course I will let you, but you need to get out of the Mercedes a block before we get there!" Ivan said with a tone of reluctance in his voice.

"So, are you ashamed of me, Mr. Rock 'n Roll?" Adrianna asked querulously.

"No. You know…it's just that…"….Ivan began to stammer and to stutter…

"It's just that you don't want that other brown haired girl friend to know about me…. the BLONDIE!" Adrianna quipped back.

Ivan scrunched up his face in chagrin and gained the courage to glance over at the 'Blonde movie star type' sitting to his right in the passenger seat of the Mercedes. It surprised him when he saw that Adrianna was smiling at him.

"What?!" Ivan declared, pleasantly surprised when he purveyed the large smile.

"I am not an idiot, Ivan. I have known about the brown-haired Katarina, the one you live with, since the first day you walked into the door at the underground nuclear research facility."

"You have?" Ivan quizzed.

"Yes, of course I have," she replied very matter-of-factly.

"But Adrianna, Katarina is just my mommy figure I am not…."

The tall blonde laughed gustily in disbelief "We will talk it about this later, love" as she patted Ivan gently on his arm and pointed toward an empty parking space on the corner a block away from RED ELVIS nightclub. "Let me out here,

Ivan" she demanded as she continually pointed to the empty space.

"Adrianna, please don't be mad at me…. trust me…it is not what you think.!"

"I am not mad, Ivan. Just do your job tonight and enjoy yourself. I will explain everything later."

"OK, Ivan said sheepishly" and with that, the statuesque blonde slid out of the Mercedes.

"Ivan, LOOK!" Adrianna yelled excitedly as she pointed up the block to RED ELVIS. There at the entrance of the new night club had to be at least 100 people milling around waiting for the doors to open.

"Oh, my goodness!" Ivan declared. "I never expected a crowd like this on the first night!"

Adrianna looked back into the Mercedes and cajoled, "Ivan, just portray yourself as the KING OF ROCK 'n ROLL as I have seen you do, and you and RED ELVIS will be a huge success!" She then gave Ivan an enthusiastic thumbs up.

"OK, Adrianna …. thank you…. thank you very much!!" Ivan had begun using that trademark expression more and more to help him channel his 'inner Elvis,' and it always seemed to work very well.

Adrianna continued to give Ivan the thumbs up and stated, "Ivan, I will be in the back cheering you on!"

"OK baby, I will see you back at the research facility."

"Sounds great! You will be awesome tonight! I just know it." Adrianna then closed the car door and slowly and elegantly walked to join the throng of folks anxiously awaiting the grand opening of RED ELVIS.

CHAPTER TWENTY-FIVE

"Whew…" Ivan sighed as he pulled the Mercedes around the corner where he could park and enter the concealed side door of RED ELVIS. While parking, the door to the night club had been opened allowing folks to flow inside. When Ivan entered the back of RED ELVIS, he was shocked to see the crowd flocked around the room. A giant smile slowly emanated over his face.

"Ivan, isn't this incredible?! Katarina screamed as she spotted him milling around in the staging area behind the performing platform. She ran and gave Ivan a huge hug. "AMAZING" was what she could get out, when he interrupted, screaming, "Oh, my goodness Katarina…. I had better be great tonight!"

Katarina glanced back over her shoulder at the milling crowd…"You WILL be, Ivan; you will be AWESOME tonight! Just perform in front of these folks like you do in our apartment every night and your show will be a smashing success!"

"Thank you, thank you very much !!" Ivan replied. Then looking out over the audience lining up at the bar and milling out in front of the stage Ivan asked… "Katarina, you going to introduce me…or how is this going to work?"

Katarina looked back over the crowd again. "Ivan, give folks a minute to settle in, have a drink, relax and then I will goon stage and introduce…. ELVIS …. Live in Russia!"

"OK. Wow, there is such a large audience tonight…...I thought there might just be 2 or 3 old drunks come in…" Then Ivan spread his hand, pointing to the large group… " I am going to the side dressing room and put on my best sequined Elvis jump suit!" With that, he slapped his hands together in joy, shook his thick black hair and declared…."Katarina, then you introduce me !!"

Katarina looked at Ivan, puzzled "You got a sequined jump suit?"

"Yep Katarina, I have a white sequined jump suit, just like the King of Rock 'n Roll himself."

Katarina clasped her right hand over her mouth and gushed happily. "Then tonight is going to be a smashing success!" skipping up and down in glee.

Ivan slipped off into the side dressing room and after a couple of minutes, emerged as the King of Rock 'n Roll in a perfectly fitted and sequined white jumpsuit! He appeared just like he had emerged from performing in Las Vegas.

Katarina took one look at Ivan standing there in his glittering attire and screamed, "Let's rock !!"

So, Katarina pushed through the crowd and walked up on the stage and began to clap her hands over her head and shouted… "Silence! Please be quiet, everyone!"

The audience who had mostly been milling aimlessly around turned their undivided attention to the beautiful brown haired woman commanding their attention on stage.

"Ladies and gentlemen, welcome to Kiev's newest AND premiere nightclub…RED ELVIS!"

The congregation politely clapped their hands in appreciation and nodded their heads up and down in acknowledgment. A few raised their drink glasses in appreciation. Katarina raised her right hand and declared, "I will not hesitate any further. So without further ado," she said, turning her countenance into total seriousness…. Here he is, straight from Las Vegas in the USA …. believe it or not… it's ELVIS….PRESLEY!!!'

Then Katarina dashed back to the stage holding area leaving the performing platform entirely empty. Her declaration that this was the REAL Elvis Presley that was going to appear in front of them grabbed them all by surprise, and so many glanced around at others in the audience, their mouths agape in shock and surprise.

Then Ivan jumped up on the stage and slicked back his thick black hair, strummed his Gibson guitar and began his sterling rendition of one of Elvis Presley's biggest hits….'Hound Dog.' Ivan rolled and slid his hips as he sang, *"You ain't nothing but a Hound Dog, cryin' all the time…."*

Katarina looked around RED ELVIS from her place behind the bar and started to clap her hands together in exhilaration. The audience was going WILD! People were dancing and singing and holding their hands and arms up toward the ceiling. Katarina thought the walls or ceiling might collapse, the response was so exhilarating.

The roar over the gyrating and singing 'Ivan Elvis' was mind-blowing, and the RED ELVIS sign over the picture window was reverberating with the loud commotion into the night. Katarina started looking around the room in an attempt to try to count the patrons present… AND….she felt the crowd approached 200. This was just so much more than what she and Ivan had anticipated!

Ivan ended his rendition of 'Hound Dog' and bowed deeply. "Thank you, thank you very much!" Ivan shouted as he took another deep bow. The crowd erupted even louder, clapping and stomping their feet, demanding and encore.

"It's now or never ..." Ivan sang as he took a step toward the crowd. Again everyone jumped and clapped their hands in appreciation and glee. The applause and adulation continued as Ivan completed his rendition. Next was 'Jailhouse

Rock,' which solicited same response… unbridled glee.

Katarina soon stayed busy just keeping folks' glasses filled with their favorite Russian vodka …Smirnoff. What a joyful evening it truly turned out to be.

After an hour of continuous performance, Ivan announced, "AND for my last performance of the evening…." which drew a disappointed response from the audience, to which Ivan waved his hand over his head and declared, "I will be back next Saturday night…we expect everyone to be right back here. That declaration drew an outpouring of applause and joy and a spontaneous chant of, "We will be back!"

Ivan then glanced back at a tall blonde- lady with a red star adorned Soviet baseball cap and began, *"I…can't…help…falling in love with you…"* The crowd again 'oohed and aaahhhed' at the wonderful bonus performance.

Ivan bowed over and over to the ovation and thunderous applause at the end of the performance.

"Thank you thank you very much…we expect everyone to tell their friends about RED ELVIS also."

It was an exhausted Ivan Hitler who walked up to Katarina as soon as the last patron left. "Wow,…what a night, Katarina!" Ivan declared after he had changed out of his white sequined jumpsuit and joined her at the side door entrance.

"Yep, Katarina declared as she held up a handful of paper money and a bag of money coins. "Wow," Ivan declared again, "have you counted it?"

Katarina nodded her head 'no.' "We will when we get back to the apartment." With that statement they walked out to the parked Mercedes and headed back to the apartment.

Ivan thought how quiet they were on the drive home after such a huge opening night success with their new business. Ivan assumed Katarina was simply exhausted as she had worked extremely hard that week just preparing the RED ELVIS, and then, on opening night, she was the sole bartender for all the Smirnoff vodka that was consumed.

They quietly parked the car and walked up to the upstairs apartment they shared.

Katarina then took center stage in their apartment and turned to Ivan… "So, who was the blonde bombshell standing in the back with the Soviet baseball hat on that you stared at and smiled at all night?"

Ivan's eyes enlarged to saucer size and replied "uh…uh," stammering without responding. Ivan was taken aback as Adrianna was there at opening night and she was the most stunning woman in attendance. "Uh well …. uh well… " Ivan continued to stammer. "I don't exactly know, Katarina," Ivan cajoled, trying to lie his way out of explaining to Katarina who Adrianne actually was.

The svelte tawny-haired model, as beautiful as any woman in Eastern Europe, stood up to her highest posture possible and shouted, "Liar, liar pants on fire!

Ivan stood like a little school kid caught with his hand in the cookie jar and nodded his head as if he 'knew nothing.'

"I am your Mother, so, to speak. As hard as I worked getting RED ELVIS ready, and as hard as I worked to keep all the patrons happy tonight...." Katarina sighed..."You never looked at me once. You never acknowledged me to the audience. "

"You are correct," Ivan stammered, "Yes, I should have introduced you to our audience. Katarina, you did such a great job."

Katarina kept her arms crossed her arms over her chest and declared, "All you did was PLAY Elvis Presley....and stare at Miss Blondie!"

Ivan dared not open his mouth and say something, as no matter what he said, Katarina, when she was this mad, would consider anything spouted by Ivan to be wrong.

Katarina stomped into the small bedroom that they had shared. She came back out to the small living room and plopped down a pillow and a sheet and blanket. "You are not welcome in the bunk bed arrangement as before. Sleep here on the couch from now on, Ivan Hitler!"

Ivan just stood in the middle of the room, his eyes wide open. Katarina had a temper, and he knew when she was mad.

"I have been your MOM for a long time, and you are required to tell me EVERTYTHING, including any love interests," she chided.

Ivan stood quietly and did not say a word as Katarina turned and walked back to the small bedroom, slamming the door hard behind her.

Ivan sighed and plopped down on his sleeping 'palace…' the hard couch, shaking his head in disbelief. "Hell hath no fury like a woman scorned…" Ivan muttered silently to himself as he looked over his new sleeping arrangement. There was only this hard couch. The upper bunk bed in the small bedroom was not all that great, but this was terrible. "OH well…." he reckoned, and he accepted his fate and pulled the sheet over his head. Before he dozed off to sleep, Ivan allowed a thought to creep into his mind…."I wonder if the real King of Rock 'n Roll has to put up with impertinence like I have had to suffer tonight?" He breathed in and out sharply, then fell fast asleep, as he was exhausted.

The next morning, a Sunday morning, Ivan arose very quietly in order not to awaken Katarina. But the lovely lady did hear him, and opened the door before he could leave the apartment

"Where you headed Ivan?" she questioned. "It's Sunday morning."

"I'm going to the research facility," Ivan replied.

"It's Sunday, Ivan," came the retort.

"I know, Katarina," Ivan replied. "We have a very important project going on that General Hartno wants me to push, so I am going in today."

Katarina was cool and simply closed the door behind her. Her continued aloofness was obvious and apparent, and Ivan wisely chose not to engage her in any further interaction.

CHAPTER TWENTY-SIX

Meanwhile, back at the White House, First Lady Pat Nixon broke the story line and explained to Elvis, "Elvis, it is here where you...and the USA get involved.

Elvis looked up inquisitively from his seat in the Oval Office. "Pat, I have been so immersed in your story...I did not hear what you just said," as he cocked his head as if to request her to state it again.

"To be blunt, Elvis, this is when Katarina Khrushchev called our CIA office and she talked to our Agent Chilon"

Elvis nodded his head in understanding.

President Nixon interrupted as he glanced down at his wristwatch from behind his desk there in the Oval Office. "Pat, the story is still long and arduous... and it will take time for what you have to tell Elvis. Pray continue..."

Pat Nixon shook her head up and down in agreement. "Elvis, I will pick up the storyline." And with that, the First Lady continued diligently, "Katarina and Ivan continued living together in that apartment, but it became very apparent that a hurdle was placed between them. Ivan got up each morning and went to the underground Russian research facility. Ivan's scientific work intrigued him immensely. The young nuclear genius stayed immersed in thought and constantly concentrated and parlayed his extreme curiosity into tangible nuclear substructures in his cerebral cortex.

Katarina left for RED ELVIS every day around noon. The night club had become a popular meeting place for locals after their work around Kiev. Then, on Friday and Saturday nights, 'Nuclear Neon Elvis' (Ivan Hitler) would show up to perform to standing room only crowds and packed houses. Word spread near and far quickly about the outstanding, captivating performances by 'Nuclear Neon Elvis.' In fact, RED ELVIS soon truly became the place to go for an after work drink OR to watch the powerful and emotionally moving live entertainment every weekend from 'Nuclear Neon Elvis.'

Some of the most powerful and prominent Ukrainian and Russian Soviet officials began to frequent RED ELVIS faithfully and regularly.

Ivan saw Adrianna every day at the research facility. They often would slide into their private alcove so they could be alone together. But Ivan did not want the blonde bombshell to attend his live performances at RED ELVIS. He was afraid that Adrianna's appearance would further upset Katarina. The lovely 'Mommy figure' was a fantastic business manager and the RED ELVIS was becoming very successful financially. He did not want Katarina and he to have a falling out, especially now that RED ELVIS was such a big hit locally. Ivan was enjoying the financial spoils and notoriety that the nightclub's success and his electrifying performances were bringing to him.

Elvis held up his hand from his seat in the Oval Office and interrupted the First Lady as he might have done in the 5th grade with his teacher at Yazoo City, Mississippi. "Sounds like kind of what happened to Priscilla and me with all of my success."

Pat Nixon shook her head in agreement. "Maybe, Elvis, but this story is about to get very, very relevant to you….and actually even more interesting. I think you will find it very relevant to you at a personal level. Pat slightly nodded her head at her husband, President Richard Nixon, to garner his agreement, whereupon the President returned the gesture in mutual acquiescence.

Elvis nodded his head in reflection of the actions of his two peers present, and said, "Please push forward with the story, First Lady….er…er again, I mean…Pat."

CHAPTER TWENTY-SEVEN

Pat Nixon smiled and continued again… clapping her hands together and saying, "Okie dokie." She jumped back to the Ivan Hitler story detailing that another reason Ivan did not want Adrianna at RED ELVIS was that Ivan had become so smitten and enthralled by the blonde he had trouble on concentrating on his Elvis routine whenever she appeared. Adrianna's appearance at the RED ELVIS would make him nervous. And Ivan was loving the spoils of success that Katarina and RED ELVIS was bringing to him.

Adrianna was fast discovering that Ivan was indeed a true genius in the field of nuclear fission and the research needed to conquer this area of expertise. Ivan was genuinely brilliant and he was incredibly driven to discover new and perhaps an enormously powerful way to split atoms to create a super powerful plutonium or hydrogen bomb.

Adrianna discovered from their intimacy that the main reason Ivan was so obsessed with this awesome discovery was so he could conquer the killers of his mother Eva and father Adolf, the country he hated and had vengeance for ……the United States of America.

So, Ivan continued his round-the-clock protocol of obsessively and diligently studying and working at the underground nuclear research facility every day….and then performing at RED ELVIS as he 'became' the one and only Elvis Presley every Friday and Saturday night.

And Katarina worked diligently to make RED ELVIS the place to go and be seen at in and around the Kiev and the Ukraine.

In due time, Ivan approached General Hartno about when he could test the preliminary version of his newly discovered, unfathomably powerful weapon. Hartno declared that he would talk with his superiors in Moscow and secure an appropriate location for Ivan to test his nuclear weapon. Ivan, being the obsessive-compulsive man he was, continued to pester the General almost every day about where…and when he could test his weapon.

Approximately three months later, General Hartno called Ivan into his office. "My superiors in

Moscow want us to load everything up on the East bound freight train to the Soviet Union's secure and extremely secretive nuclear testing site in the frozen tundra in far off Siberia!"

Ivan nodded his head and smiled broadly. "Yes, General. I understand. Sounds great."

"When do you think you will be ready, Ivan?" the General asked.

"Well, I will need Adrianna to help me get everything together to load and travel via the freight train."

Hartno nodded his head in agreement. "Adrianna is here to help you, Ivan. Sounds good."

Ivan quickly agreed and said excitedly, "With Adrianna's help, I imagine I can download everything out of the accelerator and centrifuge that I need and...." Ivan looked up toward the ceiling and rocked his head back and forth as he thought pensively. "Possibly in 10 days we will be ready to go."

"Great Ivan, I will clear everything with Moscow and we will load everything you need on the train, and we will proceed to the testing site in Siberia."

"Then I…and Adrianna…will have to unload everything off the train and reassemble everything in Siberia to pull off the big explosion!"

"Yes. Great plan, Ivan." General Hartno exclaimed. "We will get everything ready."

True to his word, it took Ivan approximately 10 days to load the freight train with the explosive elements and all necessary equipment needed to detonate Ivan's new nuclear weapon in Siberia.

After working exhaustively to ready and load everything, Ivan did not look forward to the task of telling Katarina that he would not be at RED ELVIS to perform that weekend. It was with trepidation that he walked up the stairs to the 2nd floor apartment to explain. He sighed and lamented softly as he wandered around the apartment.

Finally, Katarina looked at him sternly and spat out, "SO…what is going on, Ivan? You are acting like a grumpy old man, walking around here so slowly and talking to yourself."

"Katarina, I won't be at RED ELVIS this weekend. In fact, I won't be around all week."

Katarina placed her hands firmly on her hips and declared, "WHAT?!!" Our patrons… oh, my goodness! Everyone will be so disappointed! So many have grown to love the show….! What's happening, Ivan?"

"I can't tell you everything …but I will be on an excursion with General Hartno. I SHOULD be back for next week's show."

"Oh, you're going to try out your new experimental project with the General?"

Ivan's face torqued in an 'I can't tell you' manner and his body shuddered slightly. "It's a secret, Katarina….you know too much already!!"

Ivan shook his body negatively, picked up a sheet, covered himself up and slammed his body down on his new bed…the couch…covering his whole face with the sheet. He immediately began to 'snore' loudly to indicate to Katarina that the conversation was over.

The night passed slowly and torturously for Ivan. He constantly peeked at Katarina's bedroom door to make sure it was shut securely. Finally he got up at 5am. He dressed quietly and slipped out of the apartment.

It was a very subdued Ivan who drove to the underground nuclear facility at Chernobyl that morning. He had always told Katarina everything. She had been his mom, teacher and mentor. This keeping secrets from her hurt him deeply.

As he exited the elevator to reach the underground facility, he was met by Adrianna. One look at Ivan and she asked "WHAT is wrong?"

'Nothing is wrong," he said dismissively. Ivan subconsciously slid both hands through his thick black hair and glanced at the blonde Adrianna and quizzed, "Are we all loaded up and ready to head to Siberia?"

Adrianna sighed gently and responded… "Yep….the freight train cars are all loaded. We are ready to go."

"OK, then…. let's head 'em up and move em' out!" Ivan declared, trying to portray an old Western characterization he had observed on a movie he had seen.

Adrianna simply shook her long blonde hair, then wrapped it up under her Soviet baseball hat. Incessantly tired of dealing with 'Mr. Moody Nuclear Genius,' Adrianna inhaled and exhaled deeply, grabbed Ivan by the elbow, and dragged him back to the open elevator doors.

When the elevator opened on the upper floor, Ivan and Adrianna were met by a waiting General Hartno. Adrianna and Ivan instinctively saluted the General respectfully. Adrianna took the initiative and declared "We are all loaded up and ready to head to Siberia as planned."

General Hartno nodded his head in respect and appreciation. "OK then, let's go!" he said as he signaled for his subordinates to move forward and load onto the train.

On board, Adrianna and Ivan retired to their compartment. General Hartno took the main cabin as the diesel powered train chugged slowly out of Chernobyl and headed to the desolate areas of Siberia where the secret nuclear testing site was. Ivan and Adrianna stayed mostly secluded during the 5-day trek.

'Woo…woo'   the freight train's welcoming whistle alerted everyone including the 'hibernating twosome' that they were approaching their destination in Siberia.

As the train slowly groaned into the station, General Hartno declared, "Wow, look at that…" as he glanced back to Ivan and Adrianna. He pointed to a ready crew of 30 soldiers awaiting them.

"General Hartno," the welcoming Lieutenant chirped, snapping to attention and saluting sharply. "We are here to help you transport all needed supplies to the outpost where we are taking you."

"Great!" Ivan declared with relief. "I truly dreaded the thought of unloading all these crates."

"Me too," the tall blonde sighed, and the duo immediately walked back to the cache of necessary supplies. The 'Dynamic Duo' began to direct the work force to the storage cars, and had the workers unload all their securely packed vital components from the train. They then began to direct the crew to start reloading the packed equipment onto flat bed trucks that were in waiting.

"Where is the destination area, General Hartno?" Ivan quizzed as he held a hand above his forehead and peered into the horizon.

General Hartno took a jab with his right hand and pointed in a general area farther East. "As I understand, it is about 15 miles in the direction of the Steppes."

Adrianna walked up and put her hand over her forehead and peered into the distance as well. "Wow, is it over there at the tower that is barely visible?"

"I believe so," the General replied as he spotted the tower.

"Then we've got to transport all these crates to that location…"

"OK, we let's make sure that all the crates are loaded and head that way," Ivan added. As he and Adrianna walked around all the flatbed trucks that were being loaded and assayed whether all the equipment they needed was packed.

"Do we really need to transport all of this equipment to the area?" Adrianna asked.

Ivan sighed, "You know me, I absolutely have to have all of my equipment here so I can monitor everything … you know how I am."

"OK, I know how you are and I understand," Adrianna nodded.

So, slowly the group of flatbed trucks left the train station and headed toward the staging area. It took 2 hours to slowly navigate the rough terrain toward the towering structure that loomed ahead. When the military caravan arrived at their destination, they had to repeat the same labor intensive, cumbersome process of unloading the equipment that they had loaded just a short time earlier that same day.

Ivan led the parade and jumped out of the truck and ran to where the unloading area was laid out. "We need to set up some tents here," Ivan declared.

The head of the unloading team declared, "Not necessary. We have brought collapsible and easy to assemble portable structures that will protect everything you brought here from the elements." True to his word, three structures were up within an hour that would house all of the equipment Ivan would need to carry out his 'explosive' experiment.

Soon all of the equipment was unloaded and placed under the portable structures. Ivan waved everyone to leave the area, as he wanted privacy so he could put everything together himself. The portable structures that were erected to house all of his equipment were perfect as far as the 'Little Dictator' could tell. The 'explosion' tower loomed 5 miles away.

"NOW," Ivan reasoned, "We have to move the most important and vital…er well…shall we say…'equipment' to the explosion tower center some 5 miles away.

"Let's get it done!" Ivan shouted out as they got back in the vehicles and resumed the parade of flatbed trucks with all of the equipment needed at the detonation tower.

After arriving at the tower and explosion center, Ivan personally and carefully guided each crate to be unloaded exactly where he needed them to be at the explosion tower. When the 'explosive device' was unloaded, Ivan alone tugged and pulled the 'bomb' to the tower and attached it to the small elevating device that lifted the 'bomb' up on the tower. When Ivan was sure that the lethal package was secure, he turned to everyone and exclaimed "OK, everyone, let's load up and get back to the command and control center," and he waved his hand in a 'forward ho' manner directing everyone back to where General Hartno stood 5 miles away.

When they arrived at the control center, General Hartno and Adrianna were standing guard behind a large earthen shield that had been excavated to protect folks during explosive detonations.

Ivan scurried around wildly manipulating dials and turning on the control equipment to make sure everything was working correctly.

After thoroughly making sure all was well and correct…Ivan pulled up a chair, collapsed into it and sighed…"Whew, that was stressful." He then leaned forward in his chair and took a glance toward the explosion tower that flickered in the sun's rays approximately 5 miles away.

General Hartno pointed to the protective earthen barrier that loomed above them and declared , "This earthen barrier with this huge lead shield was built to protect us from any possibility that we might be harmed by the atomic blast."

"Boy, I sure hope it is strong enough, "Ivan declared from his seat.

"Is all of your equipment setup compatible with the control center here?" the General queried.

Ivan nodded his head…" That is my last checkup now….I believe so…but I will double and triple check to make sure the detonation center is compatible with my equipment.

So Ivan got out of his chair and scurried around manipulating dials for about 45 minutes. "We are set," Ivan declared as he clapped both hands together and smiled broadly.

"All seems good, General Hartno!" the black haired nuclear genius declared. "And what is remarkable is that this control center is almost identical to our training and preparatory area and the nuclear research facility in Chernobyl."

"Exactly Ivan, it was designed to be that way!" General Hartno exclaimed, nodding his head up and down in excited acknowledgment.

"General Hartno…and Adrianna…" Ivan stated deferring to the blonde as well… "this test will be only 1/10 the strength of the plutonium bomb that I have planned, SO…we …and the crew here should be safe behind this large earthen and lead barrier. Ivan slapped the formidable lead plate that covered the control panel area and the rest of the detonation center. "Now, let's get to the business at hand…." Ivan unthinkingly gave a 'Hitler' salute before jerking his hand away and giving a more palatable Soviet style salute. Then Ivan pointed to a group of chairs located behind the shield. He walked over to the control panel and began to flick and turn dials and knobs, readying for the transmission of the signal to detonate his new atomic device located on the tower 5 miles away. He used the small equipment portable devices he had brought from the Chernobyl area to double check the control panel at the Siberian location. Finally, he turned to General Hartno and Adrianna, "We are going to be able to view the detonation from this small television with a remote camera, I set up at the tower site." Ivan pointed to a small TV receiver that when he turned it on actually, gave a view of the explosion tower.

"Really…?" Hartno and Adrianna quizzed. Ivan nodded his head in the affirmative. "Yep, we should be able to see most of everything as it proceeds. Tell me when everyone is ready." Ivan looked at Adrianna and the General as well as about eight other folks that the General had asked to be present and to view the demonstration.

Ivan glanced again at General Hartno… "Ready, General…?

The General gave Ivan an affirmative nod indicating that he was ready for the demonstration to proceed.

Ivan glanced at "Ms. Beautiful' Adrianna and smiled, and then, with his extended right index finger, slowly, surely and deliberately pressed the bright red detonator button of the control panel.

Moments passed; it seemed as if a full minute before the group began to see a small 'plum' of explosion arise from the distant tower.

Ivan glanced at the meter he had brought from the underground Chernobyl research facility and had installed at the permanent control center in Siberia. The meter was oscillating and recording data wildly. Ivan took a step back with a concerned look on his face.

Adrianna left her seat and jumped up by Ivan. Whispering quietly in his ear in the blonde asked, "What is it, Ivan? What is wrong?"

Ivan glanced at the control center and the meter he had brought from Chernobyl. He glanced briefly at the TV monitor located at the detonation tower and then took time to actually physically step aside a second to look directly at the tower.

"Adrianna..?" General Hartno quizzed, wanting to know if something was wrong. The blonde looked back at the General and just gave a shrug and promulgated a look on her face that clearly meant...'I don't know.'

Turning back to the control center and the wildly oscillating dial on the portable meter, Ivan turned first to Adrianna then to General Hartno and screamed, "DUCK !!"…"Hide"…"Take Cover !!"

Ivan grabbed Adrianna by the arm and grabbed General Hartno by the shoulder and pulled the shocked duo under the awning of the protective earthen and overhanging lead awning that was built to protect the observers. He screamed at Hartno and Adrianna as loud as he could …."GET AS CLOSE TO THE PROTECTIVE LEAD WALL AS YOU CAN….AND HOLD ON !!" Then Ivan got behind both General Hartno and Adrianna and pushed them and pressed them as 'flat as pancakes' against the leaden wall as he could and squeezed them tightly. Adrianna turned around and gazed at Ivan in a terrified state of shock.

"Guys, the atomic explosion is going to be at least ten times stronger than I ever imagined it could be !!" Ivan pointed at the meter and jabbed his index finger at the oscillation of the hand on the 'seismograph of the explosion. "HOLD ON!!" Ivan could feel both Hartno and Adrianna 'trembling' under his grip and he pressed them even harder against the protective wall. The trio waited in terror and anticipated the atomic blast 'tidal wave' that was certain to wash over them.

'S W O O S H! 'the winds and debris cloud that swept over Ivan, Adrianna and General Hartno was like a level '5' Hurricane.

As the first wave passed, Ivan screamed "It will be the B A C K W A S H that is going to be terrible!!" And sure enough, the implosion of super-heated air, dirt and debris that rushed back in to take the place of all the air and oxygen that had been displaced by the Herculean explosion was 'surreal.'

The winds swirled and crashed against them, and as there was no lead protective panel to guard them against the 'backwash' implosion of winds, Adrianna, Ivan and General Hartno just had to hold onto each other and survive the 'Hurricane' type onslaught that bombarded them for what seemed like an eternity.

CHAPTER TWENTY-EIGHT

When the backwash 'air tidal wave' died down and was quieted away after at least 60 seconds of time or so, the stunned trio shook their heads and wiped dust and dirt from hair, faces and clothing. Adrianna, Ivan and Dr Hartno looked at each other in 'shock and awe.'

Ivan's ebony hair was plastered back against his head and created a pompadour. Adriana's blonde locks were frozen straight back, and General Hartno's short military 'buzz' cut actually made it look as if he were almost bald.

All three faces were wind burnt and had an almost 'cherry red' appearance.

Ivan shook his head in disbelief. "I knew I had come up with a very, very powerful weapon....BUT..."

Ivan first looked at Adrianna then at General Hartno. The threesome's faces were covered with black residue and tiny bits of ashes.

"The IVAN HITLER ATOMIC BOMB is unequaled in human history in power, force and destructive ability…..!!!!!" Ivan shouted as he reached out and grabbed General Hartno's hand and shook it forcefully. Then he saluted the General with vigor and dynamism. Then, because he couldn't control his manic enthusiasm, jumped a bit on one foot and gave a 'Heil Hitler' salute.

Ivan took one look at Adrianna's windswept appearance, and just as if in a Hollywood movie, grabbed the blonde, and kissed her mouth as he bent her backward. When Ivan released the smiling and giggling Adrianna, he looked skyward and gave a 'Heil Hitler' salute again and declared, "ALL I need is SIX ICBMs ...ONE FOR EACH CONTINENT… and with the Hitler Nuclear Bomb for each missile then … I… Ivan Hitler, son of Eva Braun and Adolf Hitler, will CONQUER THE WORLD ….and…..………I …Ivan Hitler…. will…… RULE THE WORLD!!!

THE END?

The answer can soon be found in:
Elvis vs. Hitler 2 (Elvis Is Alive 5)

ELVIS vs. HITLER
(ELVIS IS ALIVE – 4)

By Robert Mickey Maughon

First Edition © 2023
RMM Productions

All rights reserved worldwide under US and International Copyright Laws and Conventions.

ISBN: 979-8-9871769-2-4

Copyright Registration #
TXu002359222

Cover Art and Editing by:
Stevan Pippin, TWG, Brentwood, TN,
under the direction of
RMM Productions

Other Novels by Robert Mickey Maughon

- **Elvis Is Alive**
- **Elvis Returns: Elvis Is Alive 2**
- **Elvis Forever: Elvis Is Alive 3**
- **New Orleans ER**
- **Bell Witch: The Movie**
- **Northern Star: A Whale of a Tale**
- **Fire & Ice: Birth of Angels**

Order through: Amazon.com or your favorite online seller or bookstore.

Thanks for reading!

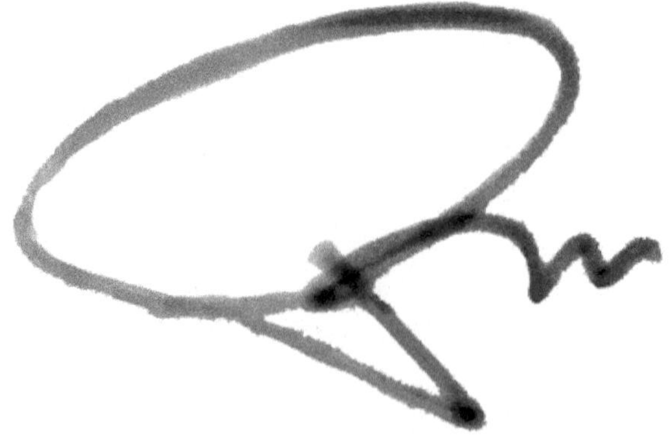

www.ingramcontent.com/pod-product-compliance
Lightning Source LLC
Chambersburg PA
CBHW040903010826
48978CB00013BB/1130

www.ingramcontent.com/pod-product-compliance
Lightning Source LLC
Chambersburg PA
CBHW040903010826
48978CB00013BB/1130